'He who owns the oil will own the World.' *Henri Berenger, 1921*

Also by Leo Kessler

The *SS Assault Regiment Wotan* Series

SS PANZER BATTALION
DEATH'S HEAD
CLAWS OF STEEL
GUNS AT CASSINO
THE DEVIL'S SHIELD
HAMMER OF THE GODS
FORCED MARCH
BLOOD AND ICE
THE SAND PANTHERS
COUNTER-ATTACK
PANZER HUNT
SLAUGHTER GROUND
HELLFIRE
FLASHPOINT
CAULDRON OF BLOOD
SCHIRMER'S HEADHUNTERS
WHORES OF WAR
SCHIRMER'S DEATH LEGION

The *Stormtroop* Series

STORMTROOP
BLOOD MOUNTAIN
VALLEY OF THE ASSASSINS
RED ASSAULT
HIMMLER'S GOLD
FIRE OVER KABUL

The *Otto Stahl* Series

OTTO'S PHONEY WAR
OTTO'S BLITZKRIEG!
OTTO AND THE REDS

The Sea Wolves Series

SINK THE SCHARNHORST
DEATH TO THE DEUTSCHLAND

Also:

As Klaus Konrad
The Russian Series
FIRST BLOOD
MARCH ON MOSCOW
FRONT SWINE

Leo Kessler

Wave of Terror

Stormtroop 7

Futura
Macdonald & Co
London & Sydney

A Futura Book

First published in Great Britain in 1983
by Futura Publications, a Division of
Macdonald & Co (Publishers) Ltd

ISBN 0 7088 2300 9

Filmset, printed and bound in Great Britain by
Hazell Watson & Viney Ltd, Aylesbury, Bucks

Futura Publications
A Division of
Macdonald & Co (Publishers) Ltd
Maxwell House
74 Worship Street
London EC2A 2EN

BOOK ONE

In Tsarist times a game of courage called *Kukushka* was played late at night in garrisons in Caucasia and Siberia. Two officers stood in adjoining rooms with an open door between. One had a pistol, the other had not. At a signal the lights were extinguished. The unarmed player opened the contest by dashing towards the door yelling '*Kukushka!*' The rules permitted him to go through it straight or diagonally, left or right, crouching or leaping. His opponent's problem was to shoot him as he came through the door.

O. Gurtner: The Myth of the Eigerwald

ONE

'*Lights!*' the tight-lipped *Luftwaffe* captain standing on the raised platform in front of the assembled troopers snapped.

A click. The big briefing room was dark instantly. Someone farted and Ox-Jo Meier, Stormtroop Edelweiss's big Bavarian sergeant-major, simpered in a high falsetto, 'Get yer naughty hand from under my skirt, you dreadful fellow you! . . . Or I'll tell Mummy this very instant!' Nobody laughed. They were too tense.

'*Then roo-ll'em!*' the *Luftwaffe* officer drew out the command and at the back of the room, the projector commenced whirring, flashing a wavering beam of silver light onto the improvised screen in front of them.

Instinctively, everyone leaned forward, blinking their eyes at the confused, rapid succession of crosses and numbers until finally they cleared to reveal the flickering outlines of a great industrial city: smoke-belching chimneys, line after line of gleaming silver storage tanks and great tangles of railway lines, gleaming in the sunshine.

'*Ploesti*,' the briefing officer snapped, tapping the poor quality picture with his pointer, as the aerial cameraman came lower showing the audience the colonnaded broad avenues redolent with lilacs and roses. 'Ploesti, Rumania. Fifty kilometres north of the capital – Bucharest.'

At the back of the room, Colonel Stuermer, the professional mountaineer commander of the élite Stormtroop Edelweiss, bit his bottom lip in bewilderment. What had this obscure Balkan city got to do with his mountain boys? The unknown cameraman continued to zoom from left to right, surveying the whole great industrial complex and finally focusing on the gleaming snow-capped mountains in the far distance.

'Ploesti is the largest oil-producing city in the whole of Western Europe,' the *Luftwaffe* officer went on. 'It started refining petroleum commercially in 1857, two years before the first petroleum strike in the USA. Now Ploesti produces ten million tons of oil annually, including 90 million of Europe's most superior octane aviation fuel.' For a moment or two the aerial cameraman lingered over the smoking stacks, cracking towers, the pumping and tank farms and, most importantly, the great modern refineries.

'Without that fuel not a single German plane would fly, nor tank move. Our own synthetic petrol industry produces a mere five per cent of our needs. Ploesti is vital to the Third Reich's war effort . . .' He let his words sink in. 'Fortunately, since 1940 Rumania has been a faithful ally of ours and Ploesti is now firmly under German control – as you can see.' He tapped the flickering screen with his pointer and as if in obedience to an unspoken command, the pictures of the city's industrial area gave way to rank after rank of camouflaged gunpits from which pointed the long, wicked barrels of 88mm flak cannon; a swarm of yellow-nosed Messerschmitts hushed by; a slow train, much like the other goods trains they'd seen, steamed along a track – suddenly the tarpaulins covering the length were thrown back revealing ugly four-barrelled 20mm cannon; barrage balloons sailed into view, tied together by formidable chains, looking for all the world like tethered elephants; a squadron of Stuka dive-bombers dropped into the screen, cannon thumping.

Stuermer looked at Greul, his harsh-faced second-in-command, and the latter returned the look. Major Greul was as impressed as he was. He, too, had never seen such formidable air defences in three long years of war. As if to confirm his thoughts, the *Luftwaffe* man barked. 'Ploesti possesses the most effective anti-aircraft defence system in Europe, indeed in the whole world. Nowhere is there a heavier concentration of flak guns and warning systems, gentlemen. Its inner line of defence of flak guns has a depth of five kilometres, its outer one of twenty-five kilometres, manned by 75,000 *Luftwaffe* troops. In addition there are 250 frontline fighter aircraft stationed around Ploesti permanently, with an additional five hundred on stand-by, plus the whole of the Rumanian Air Force, the Bulgarian Air Fleet and—' He broke off suddenly, gasping for breath. 'Gentlemen, I won't bore you with the details. The question you must be asking yourselves at this moment is—'

'When do the dancing girls with the naked tits come on!' Jap, Sergeant-Major Meier's half-breed running-mate broke in.

'Quiet there!' Greul barked angrily. Prig that he was, he never understood that the troopers' crude attempts at humour were their way of relieving tension.

Stuermer nudged his second-in-command. 'Let it go, Greul,' he whispered. 'Let it go.'

'Dancing girls with naked tits,' the *Luftwaffe* officer echoed cynically. 'Gentlemen, if you have any stomach for such things after what you will see in a few moments, I will gladly pay for the services of a high-class Berlin whore for any one of you - out of my own pocket! Projectionist, *continue*!'

Abruptly white streaks erupted across a dark sky. Stuermer strained his eyes. He could just make out the squat black shapes of bombers, many bombers, crossing the screen in great extended 'V's. The cameraman zoomed closer. Fat silver shapes loomed into view, large white stars marked on their metal rumps, the sun glistening on the perspex gun blisters that were everywhere.

'B-24s,' the *Luftwaffe* officer explained. 'American B-24 four-engined bombers. The British call them Liberators. The Tommies dearly love such cheap propaganda devices, I'm afraid,' he sneered. 'They'd rather fight the war with words than weapons, it seems.'

One of the giant bombers was transfixed by the cameraman at very close range. It filled the whole screen, its silver sides bristling with machine-guns, a deadly, sinister-looking machine of destruction.

'*Babe, the Big Blue Ox*,' the *Luftwaffe* officer read the plane's name painted on its side just underneath the cockpit next to a garish sketch of a massive ox. 'It is a bit ox-like, isn't it,' he commented. 'At that particular moment last year it was carrying 2,150 kilos of bombs, bullets and thermite sticks, all intended for Ploesti.' He chuckled in the glowing darkness. 'Fortunately for our oil supplies, that plane didn't reach its destined target. Let us see just how that ox was felled.'

The film changed to a hectic jumpy series of poor quality shots, their edges dark and jagged. Stuermer recognized them immediately. They were pictures taken by the cannon cameras of a fighter plane synchronized to start filming at the same time that the pilot fired his guns.

Suddenly, great pieces of metal started to fall off the hide of the great lumbering silver whale. There was a puff of white smoke from the nearest engine and in an instant it was streaming fire, the prop motionless. Another engine on the other wing whirled to a stop. The great bomber started to sink and Stuermer, gripping the sides of his seat with sudden tension, imagined the frantic pilots desperately trying to hold their plane in the smoke-peppered air, as the German fighter came in for the kill.

The American gunners in the side and upper turrets were now hosing the path of the approaching killer with tracer, which seemed to hurtle towards the cannon cameras like a moving wall of hailstones. But there was no stopping the fighter. His pumping cannon ripped great gleaming holes the whole length of the fuselage, tearing the crude picture of a bull to shreds. A gunner slumped over his gun, his turret shattered, the perspex transformed abruptly into a gleaming spider's web. Something dark fell out of the bottom of the plane. 'Rats abandoning the sinking ship,' the *Luftwaffe* officer commented cynically, as the dark shape became a man and the hump on his back was transformed into a great white canopy of billowing white.

Stuermer gasped. The parachute snapped on the tail wheel. Now, as the B-24's nose started to tilt with grim inevitability into its final dive, the lone man hanging to the tail at two kilometres above the earth fought frantically to free himself before it was too late. He was unsuccessful.

The scene changed. Suddenly the sky was transformed into a confusion of bombers and fighters; yellow-nosed Messerschmitts attacking; B-24s smoking, burning, spinning down like giant metallic leaves. Two planes collided and erupted in a great ball of flame. Streaming black smoke and fiery flame, friend and foe inextricably intertwined in death whirled down to the tilled checkerboard of the Rumanian countryside. A lone man, his knees clasped to his head, revolving like some ace diver in a triple somersault, came whirling through the confusion to be hacked to pieces of raw meat by the whirling propeller of a B-24. A Liberator exploded. For a fleeting second the whole screen was filled with the brilliant blinding flame of a great and tremendously violent explosion. When it cleared, all that remained of the plane were four balls of flickering fire – the fuel tanks – which were quickly consumed as they fell to the green carpet below.

The spectacle registering on Stuermer's eyes at that moment was so fantastic that his brain turned numb to the horror of that silent death and destruction flickering before him on the soundless screen. He sensed, too, that his troopers were experiencing the same sensation; for the hush which had descended upon the hot projection room as the killing had commenced in that far away Balkan country told all.

The minutes passed. Horror after horror. Fighters exploding. Parachutes, white and yellow streaming away through the debris which flooded the sky. Great bombers suddenly dropping out of the heavens to go plunging to their death below. And then the worst horrors of all. The pictures of the dead – charred, hideously mutilated, lying among the shattered smoking wreckage of their planes, some reduced to the size of babies by the tremendous heat; others ripped apart with their entrails crawling out of their bellies like horrible obscene worms; many almost unrecognizable as human beings, their limbs severed and scattered about them in the fields; and finally, a lone head, complete with pilot's leather helmet and, attached radio lines, staring upwards at the group of awed Rumanian peasant-farmers, their honest, humble faces contorted with fearful disbelief.

The projector ceased running. For one last instant that severed head, filling the whole screen, stared at the numbed spectators before the nightmare vanished and the room was plunged into darkness.

'Kunze, lights!' the *Luftwaffe* officer's sharp incisive voice cut into the heavy awed silence.

The lights snapped on and set the Edelweiss troopers blinking and rubbing their eyes while the handsome *Luftwaffe* officer stared at them with a twisted grin on his lean face. 'Well, anyone want the services of a high-paid Berlin whore now?'

No one answered. Big red-faced Ox-Jo glared at the officer, but he kept his tongue to himself and even Jap, his wizened, yellow-skinned running-mate, remained silent.

'Thus the first attempted American bombing raid on the Ploesti oil refineries in June 1942,' the *Luftwaffe* captain cleared his throat and dropped his pointer. 'It was, needless to say, gentlemen, a complete and total failure.' He took one last glance around the tough, weathered faces of Germany's élite climbers, who since the invasion of Norway had been called upon by the High Command time and time again to carry out special and hazardous missions for the Führer, 'But they will undoubtedly . . .'

From the door a well-known harsh voice beat him to it, 'They will come again – this year!'

The bemused troopers swung their heads round as one, startled at hearing *that* voice here. An enormously fat figure blocked the entrance to the room, his tremendous chest and belly covered in a bright pink uniform of a kind that none of the gaping soldiers had ever seen before, the right breast glittering with a myriad decorations and orders.

Major Greul, the Edelweiss's only Nazi, was the first to

recover from the sight of this sudden apparition. He sprang to his feet and clicked his heels together smartly. His right arm shot out rigidly. *'Heil Herr Reichsmarschall!'* he bellowed, as everywhere the startled soldiers shoved back their chairs and stumbled to a position of attention.

'Great crap on the Christmas Tree!' Ox-Jo whispered out of the side of his mouth to Jap, 'It's his nibs – it's Fat Hermann himself!'

At the door Reichsmarschall Hermann Goering raised his jewel-encrusted marshal's baton to his berouged cheek in acknowledgement, a smile on his lipsticked lips, and said, 'Gentlemen of Stormtroop Edelweiss! I have a mission for you.'

Colonel Stuermer's heart sank.

TWO

Goering toyed with the handful of uncut diamonds, running them in and out of his brightly lacquered nails like a Greek with worry-beads, while the bewildered men of Stormtroop Edelweiss filed out of the room to leave him alone with Colonel Stuermer and Major Greul.

But in spite of his gross bulk and effeminate appearance, the *Reichsmarschall* was still the same shrewd judge of men that he had once been when he had commanded the Richthofen Fighter Squadron in the First World War, one of Imperial Germany's most decorated and daring fighter aces. For now as he stared at the tall young officers, with their weathered, bronzed faces and the typical hairline wrinkles around the eyes that indicated the professional high peak climber, he knew he could not have two more suitable men for the bold task he had thought up for Stormtroop Edelweiss.

He knew that Stuermer, who had climbed everywhere before the war, was no National Socialist. But he knew, too, that the harshly handsome Colonel was a born leader of men who had proved himself on half a dozen impossible missions and one who was worshipped by his men.

The other, Gottfried Greul, was, his informants told him, a fervent Nazi. Greul did not climb mountains as Stuermer did because 'they were there'. He climbed to conquer, to show to the decadent Western world the strength, the power, the invincibility of the new National Socialist Germany. From that day in 1931 when he had conquered the North Face of the Eiger as an 18-year-old Hitler Youth and shocked the Swiss by planting the hated Nazi flag on its summit, Greul had regarded climbing as a political act:

the conquest of each new mountain as a symbol of the strength of the new German creed.

Ox-Jo Meier paused at the door, looked significantly at his CO, and then closed it. Goering and the two mountain troop officers were alone. For a moment there was no sound in that hot airless room, save for the muted bark of the drill instructor on the square outside crying: 'Well, you bunch of Christmas Tree soldiers, I'll teach you where left and right are, or crapping well die in the crapping attempt! By the Great God and all his red triangles, I swear I will. Now then, once again . . .'

Greul frowned. Stuermer smiled and Goering said, 'Things never change do they, gentlemen? I can well imagine that similar instructors have been shouting obscenities at similar dull-witted recruits on that square out there for over a hundred years or more.' He smiled at the two tall mountaineers, his small eyes almost disappearing in that mass of berouged flesh. Then he was businesslike again. 'I am sure, gentlemen, you are both wondering why you and your unit were summoned back to Berlin so hurriedly from the Finnish front. You know as well as I do that we need every mountain unit we can find, up there in the tundra. But our Führer, Adolf Hitler—' Greul stiffened automatically at the mention of the Leader's name and Goering smiled his approval and continued, 'gave me special permission to have Stormtroop Edelweiss released from the High Alpine Corps for a mission I proposed to him.'

'In connection with the film about Ploesti we have just seen?' Stuermer broke in, as always hating this oblique mystifying approach that politicians and high-ranking generals seemed to love, as if it gave them pleasure to be able to manipulate people in their presence.

'Yes, *Herr Oberst*.'

'But what use would Stormtroop Edelweiss be in Rumania, *Herr Reichsmarschall*?' Stuermer protested. 'Ploesti must be at least a hundred kilometres away from the Transylvanian Alps – and besides they are firmly in the hands of the Rumanian Alpine Corps in case the Russians attempt a breakthrough in that direction. What purpose could we serve there, sir?'

Goering savoured the moment, automatically tumbling the gleaming gems from one pudgy beringed hand to the other. 'But, my dear Colonel, the mission I have proposed for you is *not* in Rumania.'

'Then where is it, sir?' Greul asked eagerly, as always oblivious to other people's feelings and attitudes, in his single-minded fervour.

Goering turned to him. 'Where? Why, Africa, of course,' he declared jovially. 'North Africa to be precise.'

For one long moment the two officers stared at him stunned, Stuermer telling himself that Rommel and his *Afrika Korps* had just been kicked out of North Africa and wondering what the place had to do with Ploesti in Rumania.

'All right, then, you bunch of banana-sucking wet-tails,' the harsh voice of the drill instructor was crying outside on the barracks square, 'when I give the word of command "advance", I want you to open yer legs – don't bc scared, nothing will fall out . . .'

'Africa, *Herr Reichsmarschall*,' Stuermer recovered himself. 'Why Africa?'

'Because, Colonel Stuermer, that is where the next attack on Ploesti will come from, and this time we might not be as lucky as we were back in June last year. Our resources are dwindling while those of those Anglo-American terrorists are growing by the month.' For a few moments Goering's fat humorous face showed fierce rage. 'Every night those bandits of the Royal Air Force come and shatter our cities and during the daylight hours they are followed by the American gangsters of the Eighth US Air Force.' He smashed one pudgy fist into the open palm of his other hand with a soft wet sound. 'And we are virtually impotent to stop them. Even if they take tremendous losses, they come again the next day because they have the resources we in Germany do not have.'

Stuermer frowned glumly. He knew what Goering meant. He had been horrified at the state of Berlin as he had caught his first glimpses of it from the slow-moving troop train. In three years of war the city had been transformed into a smoking heap of brick rubble and grotesquely twisted metal girders, with whole sections of the working-class suburbs razed to the ground, turned into a stone desert in which the survivors lived like cave dwellers. 'So,' Goering continued, his good humour restored as quickly as it had vanished, 'The Führer and I agree we cannot run the risk of allowing the Anglo-Americans to reach Ploesti this year in view of their greater resources. In the summer the Führer plans a great offensive in Southern Russia which will undoubtedly regain the initiative for Germany. But, gentlemen, the success or failure of that offensive depends entirely on the fuel coming from Ploesti. We can't take the chance of losing that supply. Hence, Africa—' He crooked a finger at the two officers, its whole pudgy length covered in expensive diamond rings, and waddled to the map board next to the cinema screen.

Obediently they followed.

With a grunt Hermann Goering reached up, his enormous buttocks bulging through his lilac, mole-skin breeches, and flung back the cover marked TOP SECRET.

A map of North Africa was revealed, covered with a rash of blue and red symbols, which Stuermer knew instinctively marked the location of enemy units, though he wondered how German Intelligence had obtained the details of them now that Rommel had been kicked out of the Dark Continent.

Goering answered his unspoken question the very next instant. 'When Field Marshal Rommel was forced to withdraw from Tripoli last month, gentlemen,' he said, 'he left behind him a small number of sleepers.'

'*Sleepers?*' Greul queried.

'Yes, that is what they are called in Intelligence circles.

Brave bold young men, equipped with long-range radio sets, who are hidden in various parts of the area, living off what they can steal or capture from lone enemy convoys or supply dumps, and who report enemy movements, units, weather etc, etc.' Goering rubbed his pudgy hand across his heavily powdered face thoughtfully and then pointed at the map. 'There is one such sleeper here, located some fifty kilometres from the Libyan port of Benghazi – a certain *Leutnant* von Ernst, a Panzer officer who was apparently recuperating from wounds in hospital when the Allies broke through. Unfit for further active service with the tanks, he volunteered to remain behind. Lieutenant von Ernst has now been living there for over two months, God knows how, but supplying us with exceedingly valuable information. Specifically concerning the Anglo-Americans presently massing in that area, obviously preparing for the invasion of Italy.'

The talking seemed to have tired the enormous Field Marshal, for suddenly and rather surprisingly he sank down on the nearest chair like some hastily deflated barrage balloon and commenced fumbling inside his resplendent tunic with trembling fingers.

Stuermer looked down at him and thought about that lone Panzer officer, separated from his homeland by two thousand kilometres or more, living from hand to mouth, hunted all the time, knowing that in the end the enemy would find him and what his fate would be – the dirty, bullet-pocked wall of some jail courtyard and the firing squad.

'Excuse me one moment, gentlemen,' Goering's voice impinged upon his reverie. With a shaky hand, Goering placed a small mirror on the table in front of him and from a blue screw of paper shook a small heap of white powder upon it. The sweat now stood out on his forehead in great opaque beads and his chest was heaving hectically, as if he might have a heart attack at any moment. Feverishly Goering took a small bejewelled tube out of his pocket and while the two officers stared down at his trembling bulk in bewilderment, he placed it just above the heap of powder, with the other end in his right nostril. He gave a quick sniff. A quantity of powder disappeared. Swiftly Goering transferred the tube to his other nostril and repeated the movement.

The transformation in the *Reichsmarschall*'s appearance was magical. The shakes disappeared instantly, as did the hectic breathing and the great beads of sweat. Once again he was the jolly fat soldier known to Germans everywhere – save for one thing. The pupils of his eyes had almost disappeared and there was an odd, almost mad, glitter in his blue eyes.

Stuermer gasped involuntarily. Germany's most senior airman, the man who would succeed the Führer if he died, had just taken cocaine. Goering was a dope addict!

If Goering had heard the gasp of surprise, he made no mention of it. Instead he continued his briefing with new animation, busily stuffing away the mirror and the tube as he did so, his fingers perfectly steady now.

'Now we, in Berlin, have received some alarming reports from our sleeper near Benghazi over the last two weeks.' He rapped the map authoritatively. 'Throughout the three years of war in the Western Desert, numerous airfields and landing strips have been built around the port by ourselves, the Italians and the British. However, only one of those fields, here to the south, was capable of handling bombers. *Now*, our sleeper reports there are six fields in the area and gentlemen,' Goering lowered his voice significantly, 'although the area is within British Eighth Army territory, those six bomber fields are manned by US airmen – *flying B-24s*!' His glittering drug addict's eyes searched his listeners' grave faces momentarily. 'So what does that suggest to you?'

Greul was first off the mark. 'Ploesti, sir,' he rapped. 'The Ami air gangsters are going to raid Ploesti from Benghazi.'

Goering beamed at him and patted the Major jovially on the back with all the fake bonhomie that was typical of him. '*Genau, Herr Major . . . genau!* It is exactly the same conclusion to which my own experts of Air Intelligence have come to. Benghazi is the place from which the Americans will launch their next raid, flying across the Mediterranean, perhaps across the toe of Italy.' Skilfully Goering traced a proposed route across the map of Southern Europe into Yugoslavia, across Bulgaria. 'And thus into Rumania. Or conversely so that they will not have to fly across the territory of our Allies, the Italians and the Bulgarians, they might swing across the territory of so-called neutral Turkey – those damned Turkish slime-shitters are working hand-in-glove with the English – out into the Black Sea and thus into Rumania.' He shrugged and his enormous stomach rode up his tunic impressively. 'My Air Intelligence are not quite certain of the route the Americans might take – there are several schools of thought on the subject, it appears. But in the final analysis, it doesn't matter, gentlemen, because if we are lucky,' Goering leaned forward significantly, 'those bombers will never take off.'

Suddenly, Stuermer felt the cold finger of fear trace down his spine, as a dark inkling of what was now to come began to form in his mind.

'How do you mean, sir?' Greul asked.

'I mean, Major Greul, that it is my intention to destroy those damned Yankee bombers before they ever start. With effect from this moment, I want you, Colonel Stuermer, and you, Major Greul, to commence actively planning an operation for Stormtroop Edelweiss to destroy those machines. You will have every resource of the *Luftwaffe* at your disposal – aircraft, gliders, our high speed rescue launches, any means of transport you select – to achieve your objective. All my experts at the Air Ministry – explosives men, intelligence officers, terrain and topography experts,' he gasped for breath, his fat face gleaming with drug-induced animation, 'are there to give you any advice and assistance you may require. Finance is no problem. I have already arranged for five thousand pounds

OPERATION 'TIDAL WAVE', THE U.S. PLAN TO BOMB PLOESTI, 1943

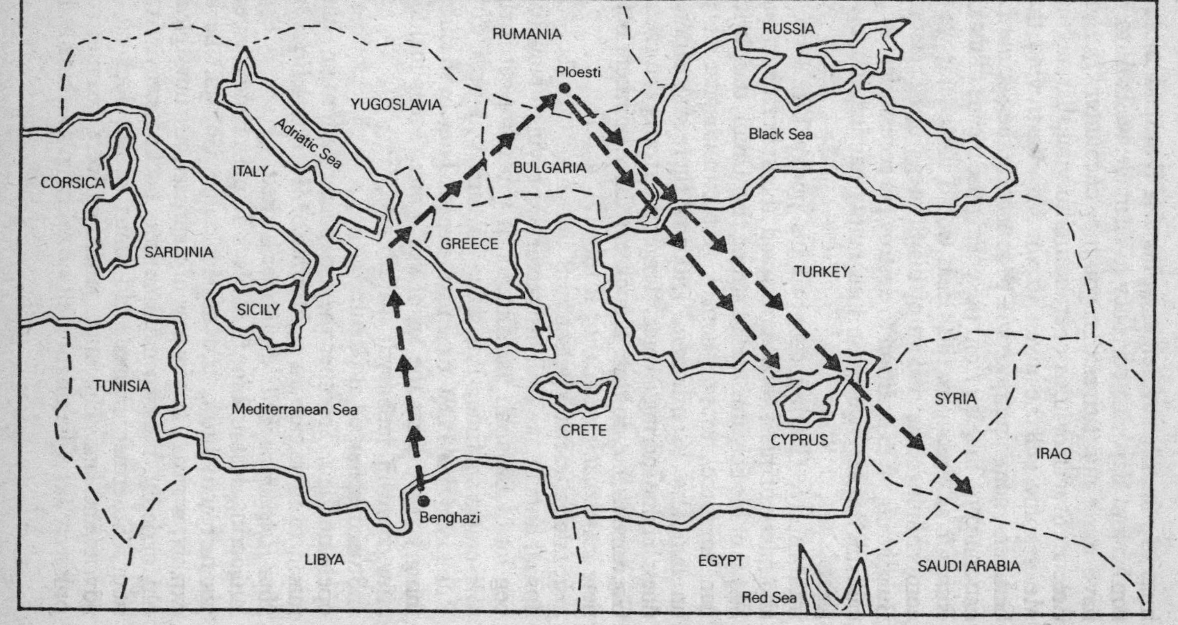

in gold, British sovereigns, plus ten thousand more in British and Egyptian currency to be made available to you for bribing any natives that you may encounter. In short, Colonel Stuermer, this operation is so vital that anything you ask for will be given to you. By destroying those bombers, gentlemen, we will be satisfying the Second Law of Strategy – to seize from the enemy the means of making war. Or as Frederick the Great would have said: we are conforming to the maxim of his Strategy of Accessories. By sending an expedition to destroy his accessories, in this case his planes, we leave him empty-handed, unable to fight.'

Abruptly, Goering dropped his pudgy hands on the shoulders of his two listeners and the sweet penetrating odour of his perfume was so strong that Greul, the puritan, had to force himself not to recoil in disgust at this unmanliness. 'Gentlemen,' and now there was a note of pleading in Goering's voice, 'forget the strategy, forget the big words. Just do this. Knock out those bombers before they *knock out* Ploesti! For if they do, gentlemen, we are lost, fatally, inevitably lost . . .'

And outside the drill instructor was crying. 'Now listen you lot of Bavarian barnshitters, if you don't get it right this crapping time, I'm going to turn you over to the Russkis in that POW cage up the road. They're so shitting hungry, they'd eat the lot of yer – *raw*, bones included. Now come on, let's try it again!'

Stuermer looked at Greul.

He nodded. Together they snapped to attention, hands raised to their caps in rigid salute. '*Mit Ihrem Erlaubnis, Herr Reichsmarschall?*' Stuermer barked.

Goering, lost in some fit of black despair, hand clasped to his furrowed brow, did not look up. 'Go, go,' he said weakly, waving a flabby paw in dismissal. 'Go now, *please*!'

Hurriedly, the two mountaineers backed away. At the door, Stuermer paused and flung a last look at the *Reichsmarschall*. His huge shoulders were heaving compulsively, as if he might well be sobbing. Looking at him

Stuermer realized just how vital Stormtroop Edelweiss's new mission was. If they failed in Africa, it could well mean the end of the Reich.

THREE

Although it was still early, the heat was intense. The glare of the bright yellow sun across the blue of the Mediterranean cut the eyes like the blade of a sharp knife. Soon the *khamseen* would arrive as it always did punctually at midday, flooding the hot yellow dust along the Libyan coastal shelf so that the parked B-24s stood deep in the stuff like elephants bathing in a tropical river.

But the men lying naked in the white burning sand of the dunes noticed neither the heat nor the glare; nor were they concerned with the hot dust wind which daily made their primitive existence in the tented Air Force camp even more miserable than it normally was. For their undivided attention at this moment was concentrated on the strange white seaplane that had come floating out of the burning sky so suddenly and was now preparing to land on the Mediterranean.

'It can't be a Catalina,' Shorty Perkins whispered, keeping his voice low, as if he thought the pilot of the plane might hear him.

'Hell, no!' Bull Bulcombe boomed in that voice which had given him his nickname known throughout the 11th US Air Force. 'The Catalina is a lot bigger than that crate.'

'Could it be a Limey job?' the Prof, weedy little Jenkins, a former instructor in German at the University of Maryland's College Park, queried in his usual precise manner.

Bull shook his massive shaven head. 'No, don't think so. All they've got operating in this area are those Sunderland flying boats of theirs and if you'd have done your aircraft recognition correctly, Prof, you'd have known the Sunderland has four engines. That job out there has got two.'

'I'll take a C-minus,' the Prof said, and the other two laughed shortly.

Behind them in the shelter of the dunes, the rest of the men from Killer Kane's Pyramiders were getting dressed after their swim in the Mediterranean – the high spot of their day – still unaware of the intruder in their remote area.

Bull shielded his eyes against the glare of the sun, trying to make out the identity of the white-painted seaplane that was obviously now going to touch down on the sea. As he did so, the muscles rippled up his bronzed, muscular arm to the line of jagged holes in his shoulder, a souvenir of an encounter over Regensburg with a German Messerschmitt. Just like the rest of Killer's old-timers, Bull Bulcombe had paid his toll in blood to the *Luftwaffe*, and like them, too, he hated the Kraut with a passion.

Suddenly, he spotted the loathsome crooked cross of the enemy; brilliant, stark, black against the pristine white of the tail. 'Kraut!' he exclaimed.

'What?' Shorty Perkins, Bull's co-pilot, exclaimed. 'What in Sam Hill is a Kraut doing over here?' It was a question which was going to occupy American Air Intelligence for the next few months. But at that particular moment, Bull was not in the mood for reflections on that particular question. In an instant he was seized by that same blinding rage that always overcame him when he spotted that hated black cross. His thick hairy fingers shot out to his forty-five which lay next to him in the sand. Killer Kane insisted they should take their weapons with them everywhere, even when they were off duty. Then he grimaced and let go. He hadn't a hope in hell of knocking out the German seaplane with a pistol. 'Goddammit,' he cursed, 'a forty-five is about as much use to me at this distance as a pecker is to the Pope!'

Shorty Perkins, a devout Catholic, shot a quick glance skywards, a look of utter dismay on his face, as if he expected Kane to be struck down at any moment for such blasphemy.

Prof grinned and said, 'What ya gonna do, Bull?'

'I'm gonna knock that bastard outa the sky,' their chief pilot grunted, his eyes glued to the white seaplane as it descended, its props already ruffling the smooth blue surface of the water below. 'That's one Kraut that's not gonna get away.' Bull stopped short. 'Did you bring the BAR with you, Prof?' he asked quickly.

Prof, who was Bull's chief-gunner, nodded. The small ex-teacher always attempted to get a practice shoot-in every day, keeping himself in training with almost pedantic thoroughness. 'Yeah, I've got it back with the boys.'

'Get it!' Bull snapped. *'At the double!'*

The Prof needed no urging. Skinny shoulders bent, thin arms working like pistons, he doubled away over the hot white sand to where the others dressed. One minute later he was running back, the automatic rifle cradled in his arms, the leather magazine container slung over his naked chest.

Bull almost pulled the infantry weapon from his arms. 'Gimme!' he snarled, flinging himself down once more in the sand, heavy muscular buttocks a startling white against the deep brown tan of his scarred back.

'Jesus, Bull, *I'm* the gunner!' the Prof started to protest, but Bull was already beginning to lead the seaplane in, the butt of the BAR tucked deep into his naked shoulder, his eye squinting along the blue metal barrel, as the German plane grew larger and larger in his sights.

The Messerschmitt which had got him over Regensburg had also come in straight to front, barrelling towards the Fortress he had been flying at 400 mph, filling the whole front of the cockpit with its evil yellow nose and black ugly shape so that he had felt it would crash right into the four-engined bomber. And then in the very last instant when it had seemed there was no hope left, violet flame had crackled the length of its wings. White flame had hurtled towards him, its burning incandescence blinding him. The perspex had shattered alarmingly. The great black shape broke to the right. Something had struck him in the arm with the kick of a mule. He had reeled back against the seat, screaming with unbearable pain, his nostrils filled with the stink of burned cordite and the hot copper smell of his own blood. Then he had blacked out.

Now, as the big Captain prepared for the kill, his face set in a wolfish snarl, his finger curling around the trigger, taking first pressure, Bull remembered that moment of utter fear and pain and knew no mercy. 'Okay, you bastard,' he hissed, taking second pressure, controlling his breathing carefully, 'take – *this*!'

The BAR kicked hard at his shoulder. To his front the air rippled suddenly. There was the stench of burnt explosive. Swiftly, Bull swung the gun from left to right. The perspex of the cockpit shattered, just as his had done over Regensburg. He grinned evilly and held his finger on the trigger, watching great pieces of metal being ripped from the plane's fuselage as it came lower and lower, blinding white glycol streaming up from the shattered port engine.

'You've got him . . . *you've got him, you big bastard*!' Prof cried excitedly, automatically slapping another magazine into Bull's outstretched hand, while Shorty Perkins crossed himself. Friend or foe, he could never overcome the sight of a plane being shot down; he always prayed for their crews.

For a fleeting moment, the blinded pilot, unseen behind the cracked gleaming perspex, tried to right the plane and it seemed as if he might do it. With its starboard engine going full out, dragging up that wing, he was obviously attempting to gain height once more and escape.

But the German pilot had not reckoned with Bull Bulcombe. Face set in grim purpose, the big hulking Captain pumped slug after slug into the seaplane. It faltered alarmingly. With an audible slap, it hit the waves. The pilot revved his single engine desperately. Twin crests of boiling white foam appeared at its floats.

'Watch him, Bull!' Prof cried exuberantly. 'He's gonna—'

The rest of his words were drowned once more by the chatter of the BAR as Bull poured a whole mag into the seaplane. The air stank of cordite. Red and white tracer stitched the blue sky. Bits of metal flew from the fuselage in a metal rain. Now thick black smoke started to stream from the region of the tail. 'He's burning!' Shorty Perkins cried, 'you've got him, Bull . . . *got him*!'

Oily smoke began to shroud the plane as it staggered forward, bumping and lurching over every fresh wave as if it were running into a solid brick wall. At over a hundred miles an hour, it roared forward out of sight beyond the dunes, leaving a trail of smoke behind it.

Bull dropped the BAR and wiped the sweat from his dripping brow. 'I don't know—'

There was a tremendous crash. A wave of hot air slapped him in the face like a blow from a flabby wet hand and snatched the air from his lungs, cutting Bull off in mid-sentence. Next instant a dark mushroom of smoke started to ascend into the blue sky.

Bull gasped for breath, while the others staggered shakily to their feet. He followed and gulped. 'Come on, you guys, let's go and have a look-see.'

Together with half a hundred other crewmen of Killer Kane's élite bomber wing, Bull doubled heavily through the ankle-deep white sand towards the spot where the plane had disappeared. Ten minutes later they found it. It had smashed – at one hundred miles an hour – into one of the rusty hulks of tramp steamers that littered the coast off Benghazi. Its front had folded back like a banana skin under the impact.

Hurriedly the excited Americans waded into the waist-deep water, the fact that this was an enemy plane forgotten now, eager to rescue any survivors.

There were none. The pilot sprawled over his shattered controls dead, his face looking as if someone had thrown a handful of strawberry jam at it. The gunner was similarly dead, transfixed by his own machine-gun which had been forced clean through his skinny chest by the impact of the crash. As for the radio operator, his body had been severed from his head by a razor-sharp spar so that now his head, supported by the radio earphones, swayed gently back and forth with the motion of the waves.

That was enough for Killer Kane's men. Suddenly their excitement vanished. They were fliers themselves; they knew this might well happen to them, too. Morose and silent, they started to wade back to the beach, all conversation ceased, their eyes still full of that terrible sight.

It was only as they plodded back to the waiting trucks which would bear them back to the Field, that Bull, in the lead as usual, noticed the line of twisting naked foot-prints – like those of a man who might have been very drunk, or very hurt – leading inland. He frowned and then on impulse bent down and ran his forefinger over one of the strange blobs of wetness intermingled with the footprints.

'What is it, Bull?' the others asked curiously, crowding in around him as he knelt there in the sand.

By way of an answer, Captain Bull Bulcombe held up his finger. It was stained a pinkish-red. 'One of them,' he said with uncharacteristic hesitation, 'one of them got away . . .'

He stared to his front. But there was nothing but the steady rolling yellow sea of the burning desert. Bull quickened his pace, mind suddenly made up. 'Got to report this to Killer,' he announced. Next moment he was running heavily across the sand.

FOUR

Colonel 'Killer' Kane sat on the eighty-man crapper of the officers' latrine – each position was made up of an old oil can – and with his olive-drab slacks around his ankles and 45 Colt in one hand ready to fight off the jerboa mice and rats which swarmed everywhere in the desert camp, his eyes fixed on the field beyond, waiting for the Liberators to appear.

He had dysentery again. But that was nothing new among the crewmen of his Pyramiders. At least half of his command suffered from it at any one time in the fly-blown, stiflingly hot tented camp.

Abruptly, Kane's craggy, tough face lit up. Now the jerboas, the rats, the state of his stomach, the misery of the desert camp were forgotten. A roar was coming from the west, growing louder and louder by the instant. This was it!

Directly out of the bright yellow ball of the sun, the five B-24s came thundering in, their twenty racing engines whipping up a great storm of brown dust behind them, as they headed for the mock target at tree-top height. He raised his free hand and shaded his eyes against the blinding, slanting rays of the sun, his mouth open to survive the shock of that tremendous noise. Now the lead bomber was directly above the circle of white, drawn in the desert two hundred yards away. The bomb doors in its fat belly swung open. The plane was so low that he could even see the scars on it where the Liberator had scraped some object or other in its daring low-level flight. Crazily a myriad wooden bombs started to tumble downwards in wild confusion. Kane tensed. Then in spite of the fresh spasm in his gut, his craggy face lit up. 'Hot damn!' he cried aloud to no one in particular, 'the sonuvabitch is right on target!'

Next instant he grabbed hold of the sides of the crapper as the Liberator roared in above his head, nearly overbalancing him in its tail wind.

One after another the others came zooming in, making the desert echo and re-echo with their noise; and each one of them dropped its bombs exactly within the target. Then they were gone, doing a ceremonial 'buzz' of the camp and undoubtedly, a suddenly happy Killer Kane told himself, breaking what remaining windows there were.

Killer Kane, who was going to be one of the three main commanders in 'Operation Tidal Wave' relaxed a moment, although his guts were rolling and moaning ominously. The low-level approach, he told himself, had to be the way, although to the man-on-the-ground it would appear he could knock the fat-bellied, four-engined bird out of the sky with a rock – it was that big. Yet the Krauts had become accustomed to the Liberators attacking from 20,000 feet up. But an unprecedented low-level strike would take the enemy by complete surprise. It would allow tremendous precision bombing on the target. It would reduce losses by presenting the enemy flak-gunners with only low fleeting targets and would mean for the first time that the gunners themselves would come under fire when their own air gunners opened up with the massed fire of hundreds of 50 calibre machine-guns. But above all, it would cheat the Kraut pursuit planes of only half their normal sphere of attack. And any of the guys who were mortally hit in combat would have a better chance at low level to skid-land than those who had been crippled at twenty thousand feet. Kane moaned softly as another spasm overcame him, but retained his smile all the same. Yes, that demonstration had just proved it. The most radical tactic was the most practical. The *coup de main* would be delivered at tree-top altitudes.

'Colonel Kane, sir!' a voice broke into his thoughts.

Killer looked up. Captain Bull Bulcombe, his most

senior pilot, towered above him, standing rigidly to attention, his hand touching his battered cap in salute.

'Goddamnit, Bull,' he roared in irritation, 'don't you try to snow me, while I'm sitting on the crapper with my hands full! For crying out loud, what next?'

Bull grinned down at his CO. 'I'm not trying to snow you, sir. Something urgent has come up, something very urgent.'

' 'Kay, 'kay,' Killer Kane said wearily, pulling up his slacks weakly, knowing that he'd be back inside the officers' latrine within the hour; for no amount of morphine and kaolin seemed to be able to stop these damned desert shits – the trots as the Limeys called them. 'What is it?'

'I've got a problem, sir.'

'Who ain't?' Killer answered morosely, holding out his hands as the Water Wallah, the Senussi Arab Wog, who cleaned the latrines came limping up with a can of tepid water clasped to his skinny side. The Wog mumbled something in his own unintelligible lingo and started pouring the precious water over Killer's hands. 'Okay, that's enough,' Killer snapped. 'Savvy, enough, we've got to save the goddam stuff.'

The Arab, who was tall and very light-skinned for a Senussi, understood the tone of Killer's voice if not the words. Obediently he tilted up his can and went about his normal task of placing neatly cut squares of the Army newspaper, *The Stars and Stripes*, at the side of each seat. Kane eyed him for a moment while he considered whether there was any point in going back to his office. He decided it would be safer to remain near the crappers and said, 'Okay, Bull, where's the fire?'

'I don't know exactly how to put it, sir,' Bull began a little hesitantly.

'Aw, come off it, Bull. Either piss or get off the pot! I've got a busy afternoon in front of me, if I can ever get away from this goddam crapper. Shoot!'

'Well, it's like this, sir.' Bull started to explain what had happened on the coast that morning. Kane listened with growing interest and apprehension, the fresh set of ominous rumbles in his sorely tried guts forgotten for a while. Behind him the Water Wallah continued about his task in his usual slow manner, passing by a waiting Shorty Perkins and the Prof.

Finally Bull ended and stared at his commander in anticipation. Kane's craggy face creased in a worried frown for a moment, then he said, 'Bull, you big lug, I think you've gotten on to something this time. Christ on a crutch,' he burst out in sudden anger. 'What in tarnation is a Kraut seaplane doing off the coast of North Africa two months after the last Kraut soldier went into the prisoner-of-war cage?'

Bull shrugged his brutal shoulders easily. 'Do I walk across the water, sir?'

Shorty Perkins moaned softly. Everyone was supposed, according to the Catholic Church, to have an immortal soul, but he wondered about Bull's because if he had, it ought to have long been burnt up the way he blasphemed.

Bull didn't notice his anguish. 'All I know, sir,' he said, 'it's strange that when we're so close to setting off on the mission—'

'Button it up, Bulcombe!' Killer Kane barked urgently, flashing a look at the bent back of the Water Wallah. 'Security around here is the world's worst as it is.'

'Sorry, sir!'

'Forget it. All right, I'll take a chance. Let's go back to my office and discuss this further, but don't be surprised if I suddenly turn tail and beat Jesse Owens belting back for this filthy crapper.'

Bull grinned. 'I know the feeling, sir. Oh, but there is one other thing,' he added, as the little band of Americans started to plod through the sand towards the tented camp.

'What is it, Bull?'

'I think that one of the Krauts must have escaped the wreck.'

Kane stopped in mid-stride and stared up at the big ex-college footballer who towered above him. 'What do you mean?'

'Well we found footprints in the sand, didn't we, Prof . . . and Shorty?' The other two trailing behind the CO and Bulcombe nodded. 'And there was blood with them. We think that one of them, probably badly hurt, got away from the crash.'

Killer Kane forgot his rebellious guts completely. 'Why the Sam Hill didn't you say so before?' he roared. 'Come on, you big dumb-bell, let's get on the stick! If we can round this Kraut of yours up, then we'll know if they're on to Operation Tidal Wave.' At the awkward double, the four of them started running through the sand towards the camp.

Behind them *Leutnant* von Ernst straightened up, his dark eyes full of alarm and apprehension. So his radio messages had got through after all! Berlin was receiving him; though, with a faulty set, he had no means of receiving Berlin. Why else would one of their seaplanes be flying off this remote coast? Berlin was trying to contact him. But to what purpose? Suddenly he remembered what the big pilot had said. *'We think one of them, probably badly hurt, got away from the crash!'*

Heaven, arse and cloudburst! Of course, he had to find the poor fellow out there in the desert, perhaps bleeding to death, before the Amis got to him. *Leutnant* von Ernst, late of Field Marshal Rommel's élite 15th Light Panzer Division, dropped his water-can, mind made up. Next instant he was hobbling towards the coast, the pain in his shattered leg temporarily forgotten. He had to find that unknown flier before the Amis did. He had to!

FIVE

In Berlin things were moving fast now, ever since the seaplane sent to contact von Ernst had vanished without trace. 'We can assume,' Stuermer announced to Greul, the day after they had received the alarming report, 'that the Americans have taken the crew prisoner. Two things will result from that.' He ticked them off with his fingers. 'One, they will possibly be alerted to what we are about. Two, they'll know of the existence of this Lieutenant von Ernst in their midst and will set about hunting for him. As a consequence, Greul, we will have to alter our plans to account for those eventualities.'

'We won't go in by sea then, sir?' Greul had countered.

'No, by air. We'll arrive at our objective more quickly and surely that way, but I'm afraid when we get there we're in for a long footslog.'

'How do you mean, sir?' Major Greul had asked.

But Stuermer had not replied. He knew now that absolute security was essential if Stormtroop was going to have the slightest chance of success in this, the most hazardous mission they had ever undertaken; for the time being he would play this one with his cards held tight to his chest.

As Goering had promised at their first meeting, the supplies were now flooding into the barracks on the outskirts of the bomb-shattered capital. In spite of the shortages which reigned everywhere in the Reich and the fact that the hard-pressed Russian front had first priority over everything else, the happy and bemused troopers of Edelweiss began to receive canned goods and special weapons of a kind they had not seen for months, even years. There was tinned black bread from Italy which would last for months; self-heating cans of British soup taken from the bodies of fallen British commandos; Hungarian salami and concentrated Danish beer powder; dehydrated egg powder and cans of spam found in shot down American bombers. It seemed as if half the Continent was being looted to supply them with the food to sustain them on their dangerous mission. As Ox-Jo, checking in the mounds of cans that would have to last eighty men for many a week, commented to Stuermer, his voice a mixture of awe and apprehension. 'By all that is holy, sir, they're really fattening us up for this one. The prisoner ate a hearty breakfast sort of thing, eh?'

'You might say so, Ox, you big rogue,' had been Stuermer's careful comment, to which he had added a moment later, noting the sudden gleam in the big NCO's bright blue eyes. 'And mind none of those goodies stick to your greedy paws.'

'Stick to my pinkies, sir?' Ox-Jo had exclaimed, all innocence. 'Now what is that supposed to mean, sir?'

'Come off it, you hairy-assed rogue. That can of Turkish coffee is worth a fortune on the black market, and you and that evil yellow pal of yours know it. So don't let us be missing anything, or else—'

Ox-Jo had given him a pained look, but said nothing.

New weapons had come flooding in to the little unit's barracks, too. There was the new British-made plastic explosive, kilos of it, all taken from the dead bodies of the Canadians killed in the Dieppe raid the previous year. With it they could destroy whole squadrons of bombers, if they were lucky. There were also the top secret airborne recoilless rifles being developed by the SS, which packed the kick of a 75mm cannon, yet which could be carried and manned by two men. There were even two collapsible motor-bicycles taken from British paratroops, which weighed less than sixty pounds, cruised for a hundred kilometres on four litres of petrol and could be packed into an ordinary grip. As Stuermer remarked to Greul after whizzing around the parade ground on one of the tiny machines at a speed of fifty kilometres an hour, 'One feels like a monkey on a stick on the damned things and they're definitely hard on the hindquarters but they'll be the ideal thing to cover our advance.'

'Advance from where?' Greul queried in a petulant voice, obviously irritated that the CO had not yet confided in him what their objective was going to be. But Stuermer pretended not to hear the question.

Ox-Jo, listening to the little interchange, nudged his running-mate, Jap, and said, 'I'm gonna get the CO an ear-trumpet if this goes on.'

Jap looked at his big broad-faced companion and asked, 'What do you mean, you Bavarian dum-dum? Why an ear-trumpet?'

' 'Cos, he's got two tin ears these days, that's why, you little yellow ape-turd. He's playing it cunning like I've never seen the Old Man play it before. He ain't telling nobody nothing.' He frowned. 'God knows why!'

Jap nodded knowingly. 'If God doesn't know, Ox, I do . . . We're off on an Ascension Day Commando[1] believe you me, and the Old Man's trying to button up the whole op right tight so that there's no leaks anyway. Mark my words, you Bavarian slime-shitter, this is going to be a one-way ticket for old Stormtroop Edelweiss if we ain't careful.'

One week after the seaplane had disappeared with still no clue to what had happened to it, Colonel Stuermer decided the men needed a rest. They had been working solidly twelve hours a day. Though as loyal as ever, they were apprehensive and uncertain, unsettled further by the tight security arrangements which prevented them leaving the Lichtenfelde Barracks and enjoying whatever tawdry pleasures Berlin could offer before they set off into the unknown.

'Greul,' he announced that hot July day, as the sun streamed brightly into the dusty 18th century barracks

[1] German expression for a do-or-die mission.

room which had once housed the soldiers of 'Old Fritz' himself.[1] 'The men need to let their hair down. Let off steam for a few hours. It'll be their last chance. We'll have a company smoker – and I think a few ladies of the town might be called for to volunteer their – er – services and speed our brave boys on their way.'

Greul, as puritanical as ever, frowned. 'I see absolutely no necessity for that sort of thing, sir. It only saps the men's strength.'

'You wouldn't, Greul,' Steurmer replied. 'I'm sure you've got lemonade in your veins – ice-cold lemonade at that.' He smiled. 'But I think the boys would be better prepared for what's coming, if they've got a few months' accumulation of – er – dirty water off their chests.'

'As you say, sir,' Greul said non-committally, and frowned once again. Obviously the proposal offended his National Socialist frugality and single-minded dedication.

'Hard as Krupp steel, as swift as a greyhound, and as tough as leather. What?' Stuermer chortled, using the old Nazi motto, and swaggered out. If his men were going to die on some impossible mission nearly three thousand kilometres away from where he now walked, he was damned sure they were going to leave their native country for the last time with something to remember it by.

'Clock in the pisspot, arse in the shit-heap, syphilis in yer heart, comrades!' Ox-Bull, drunk on both beer and good humour, bellowed, and raised his half-litre stein. 'Sink it behind yer neckties. *Prost . . . EX!*'

Those who could still do so stumbled to their feet, and along the benches laden with good food and bottles of schnaps the 'dead soldiers' raised their stone beer mugs and replied to the toast. '*Prost, Ox . . . EX!*'

There was a momentary silence, broken only by the sound of fifty odd men guzzling beer, trying to outdo each other in an attempt to sink one half litre of good Dortmund suds in one breath.

[1] Nickname for Frederick the Great of Prussia.

As usual Ox-Jo was first. With a deep gasp, he slammed his mug down on the wet, littered, trestle table and after belching appreciatively, said thickly, 'Well, it ain't exactly Munich beer, but it's damned better than gnats' piss any day.'

'Did you know that fishes fuck in water?' Jap said apropos of nothing, as he collapsed at Ox's side, his dark Asiatic eyes badly out of focus.

'Now there's a useful piece of information,' Ox bellowed. 'It just goes to show how badly I was brung up. They made me drink water till I was two years old before I started on the beer.' He shook his head in mock sadness. 'The humiliation and misery of it all. It's surprising, I did never get a pregnancy of the stomach tubes from all that fish fucking.'

Stuermer, nursing a glass of schnaps, happy that his sweating, drunken men were happy, shook his head. How often had he attended such drunken smokers in these last few years, listening to the same old jokes and alcohol-laden toasts in smoke-heavy rooms! Yet it was these simple men who bore the brunt of the generals' decisions, decisions made at remote headquarters like moves in a kind of lethal chess game. Suddenly his heart went out to his bluff, simple, red-faced mountaineers. For he knew what lay before them.

'Did you hear the one, comrades,' Ox-Jo bellowed above the noise, 'about Fat Hermann and the flood at the Air Ministry? When his adjutant came rushing in to shout, "*Herr Reichsmarschall*, there is a flood at the Ministry. The first floor is already under water," old Fat Hermann who loves his uniforms, as you all know, said calmly, "Better lay out my admiral's uniform with the medals, I suppose!" '

'Yer,' Jap cried among the laughter, 'and do you know they're gonna design a new uniform for him. It's gonna be made of transparent plastic so he can walk around Berlin in it and show the starving civvies what real meat looks like . . .'

Stuermer laughed softly and flashed a glance at Greul,

still nursing his glass of schnaps. His face was set in a look of dark disapproval. The Major knew that virtually everything and anything was tolerated at a company smoker, even attacks on the Party *prominenz*. But Stuermer could see he didn't like it, he didn't like it one bit.

Stuermer reached for his peaked mountaineer's cap with its silver edelweiss badge on one side. 'Come on, Greul, before you have a heart attack. Let's get out of here and leave them to their jokes – and the pavement pounders. The ladies of the night are due to arrive within the hour.'

'Yessir. Of course, sir,' Greul agreed hastily, obviously glad to be relieved of the misery of this rude common evening with the men.

Ox-Jo, as senior NCO, flashed them a look from the head of the long table where four or five 'beer corpses' were already sprawled, snoring heavily.

Stuermer shook his head. He did not need to bring the men to attention.

Stuermer closed the blackout curtain carefully and paused for a moment to take a deep gulp of clean night air. It was a perfect night, the sky a pale velvet, warmed by the yellow glow of a harvest moon. A real bomber's moon, he told himself, staring up at the heavens, as the capital's searchlights poked their silver fingers into the sky, parting the few clouds, searching assiduously for the bombers of the Royal Air Force which would surely come on a night like this. Suddenly the sight reminded Stuermer of their mission and, quickening his pace, he said, 'Come on over to my quarters for a nightcap before you turn in. I've got something to tell you.'

The nightcap didn't appeal to Greul, but something about Stuermer's tone intrigued him. Instinctively, he knew that the CO was going to tell him the final details of the great mission. He quickened his pace too, while far, far away to the west of Berlin came the first shrill moan of the air raid sirens. 'Bomber' Harris's men were on their way[1].

[1] Air Marshal Harris, wartime head of the RAF's Bomber Command.

Stuermer tossed his cap on the bunk bed and crossed over to the plain wooden table on which stood the bottle of looted English whisky which Goering had sent him together with a case of cigars and a kilo of bean coffee. 'You want one, Greul?' he asked, fixing himself a good one with a dash of water.

'No thank you. I find alcohol slows my reactions.'

Stuermer shrugged. 'As you wish.' He seized his glass and sat down opposite Greul in the small room, lit by a sole naked electric light bulb. From a long way off came the first faint rumble of the flak. 'I suppose you know why I've called you over here tonight?'

'I can guess, sir.'

'Well, we leave within the next forty-eight hours. I thought it was time to give you the final details of the plan which was approved by the *Reichsmarschall* this morning.' Stuermer took a sip of his whisky and told himself the civvies were going to take a pasting again this night. It was fortunate that the Berlin-Lichtenfelde barracks were to the east of the capital, an area not often visited by the RAF. Then he began. 'We can assume now that the Amis will be expecting us – if the crew of that seaplane talked, and I see no reason why they shouldn't have.'

'I agree, sir. Those air gangsters would stop at nothing. They are all a bunch of criminal sadists!'

Stuermer ignored Greul's angry comment. 'The question is *how* and *where* will the Amis be expecting us. My reasoned guess is that they will expect us to use the front door into Africa.'

'The front door, sir?' Greul echoed, as the thunder of the 88mm anti-aircraft guns rolled ever closer.

'Yes, they will expect us to land somewhere on the coast in front of Benghazi either by boat or by air. But if they *are* expecting us to come in that way, we are not going to do them that favour.'

'We aren't, sir?'

'No, instead of using the front door, we're going to use

the tradesmen's entrance. We're going to go in by the back door.'

The room shook suddenly as the first stick of British bombs exploded somewhere in the capital's western suburbs. 'Damned air pirates!' Greul grumbled. 'But one day soon they will be paid back tenfold once the Führer's promised secret weapons come into action. Then London will suffer.'

Stuermer ignored the comment, for he wasn't so sure that those vaunted secret weapons that the Führer was always promising the hard-pressed German people, weren't merely an invention of the fertile, devious mind of the Poisonous Dwarf.[1] 'And where exactly is the back door, sir?' Greul forgot the RAF and the German V-weapons.

Stuermer crossed to his bunk and pulled a file of maps from beneath it. He flipped through them until he found the one he sought. 'North Africa,' he said, spreading it out in front of Greul, who leaned forward curiously, as the lights flickered alarmingly, as if a power station somewhere or other might have been hit by the enemy bombs. 'According to what Air Intelligence can find out, most of the enemy forces are being massed on the coast in preparation for the landings in Europe. The whole stretch of this hinterland is supposed to be empty.' His big brown capable hand swept over the territory beyond the Mediterranean coast. 'Save for a few support troops and the occasional patrol – and, naturally, the Arabs. Now, if we can reach that area, I think we should be able to make our objective without too much difficulty, and take them by surprise.'

Greul peered in the flickering light at the map. The further one looked from the coast the more sparse the names on the map became, until they finally petered out altogether to where the legend *unexplored* was printed. He bit his bottom lip in doubt. Stuermer saw the look and said quickly, 'I know what you mean. But it isn't as bad as you think. Both our own *Afrika Korps* patrols and, naturally,

[1] Dr J. Goebbels, Nazi Minister of Propaganda.

the Tommies with their Long Range Desert Patrols, penetrated deep into that unexplored area between 1941 and 1942, so we do know a bit more than is printed on this map. Some five hundred kilometres due south of Benghazi, just about here,' he indicated the spot on the empty yellow mass of the map, 'there is supposed to be a large range of sand hills, some of them reaching more than a thousand metres. Several of Rommel's patrols reported seeing them in the far distance. Thereafter – here – there is the western fringe of the Great Sand Sea reaching right up to the coastal depression, just here. As you can see, if one follows a direct route from the sand hills to Benghazi, there are only a few native hamlets, though, according to Air Intelligence, there is a good chance of encountering Arabs at these oasis spots which you can see – here, here and here. And again according to Intelligence, the Senussi Arabs who inhabit the area and fought the Italians back in the twenties are basically anti-German, though they are thought to be easily convinced of the righteousness of our cause – for a consideration,' Stuermer made the gesture of counting money with his thumb and forefinger.

Greul's lips curled up in a sneer. 'Typical, Colonel. Those black baboons are all the same. They have no honour like we Germans have. But may I ask you a question?'

'You may, Greul,' Stuermer answered, raising his voice, for now the bombs were thundering down at regular intervals and the light bulb was dancing wildly, casting crazy, magnified shadows on the walls of the little room.

'I assume that you are visualizing those sand hills – if they exist – as our DZ?'[1]

Stuermer nodded. 'In a way, I have. Go on.'

'Well, sir, what if enemy radar picks us up before we ever get there? What chance will we have then?' Greul bit his bottom lip, as if it were unfair to ask a question which might place doubt upon the success of the operation.

'I take your point, Greul, and it is one that I have

[1] Dropping zone.

discussed seriously with Goering. Surprisingly enough, our fat Marshal came up with a solution to the problem when I had just about given up on it.'

'He did?'

'Yes.'

'And what was the *Reichsmarschall*'s solution to the problem, sir?'

'Gliders, Greul.'

'Gliders?'

'Yes, those big Dornier troop transporters. As Goering sees it, we could be towed to within sixty kilometres or so of the coast. Naturally, enemy radar will pick up the towing planes. But by the time the enemy starts to scramble, the towing planes will have turned back for their bases in Sicily and the two Dornier gliders will go sailing on silently and undetected by radar to their objective.'

Greul swallowed hard. 'But, sir, at a rough guess they'll have six hundred kilometres to cover before they reach the desert sand hills you mentioned previously. That is a tremendous distancc to cover in a large glider laden with some forty men.'

Now it was Stuermer's turn to look worried. 'I agree, Greul, I agree. But Goering assures me that it is possible and he *has* allotted Edelweiss two of Germany's most famous professional pre-war glider pilots – both long distance record holders – for the operation.' He took a breath and continued. 'Both of them took part in the Eben Emael[1] op. back in forty. So they are the élite of the para corps. If anyone can pull it off, it will be them.' Stuermer's voice suddenly lacked confidence, as if for the first time he had just realized the magnitude of the task ahead.

'I don't want to paint the devil on the wall, sir,' Greul said slowly, as the bombing now started to die away and the first faint wail of the 'all clear' could be heard. Berlin

[1] In 1940, daring German glider pilots crashed their craft, laden with paras, directly onto the main Belgian fortress at Eben Emael, which guarded the vital Albert Canal. See L. Kessler: *SS Panzer Battalion* for further details.

had taken its punishment for the night. 'But it seems to me that we have little chance of success under these circumstances. You know I am prepared to die for my Fatherland and Führer.'

'Yes, yes,' Stuermer said impatiently. 'I know that, Greul, but do get on with it, man!'

'Well, sir. First, the Amis know we are coming. You agree on that yourself. Then we are going to attempt to cross six hundred kilometres of enemy-held territory in gliders although we presumably know little of the local thermals, prevailing wind conditions etc. etc., all the things that a long distance glider pilot must know *in advance* if he's going to make a success of the job. Finally, *if* we manage to fool the Amis, and *if* the glider pilots manage to cover those six hundred kilometres, then we are faced with several hundred kilometres of uncharted or relatively unknown desert, which we can assume is basically hostile to us.'

Stuermer nodded gloomily. 'Yes, of course, Greul, one has to be realistic about these things. You are naturally quite right. But we've got to go ahead whatever the risks. Why? Not in stupid corpselike obedience to orders from our superior officers, but because of that!' With one quick movement he had risen from his chair and swept back the blackout curtain. '*Look!*' he commanded.

Berlin was afire again. The whole horizon to the west was a sea of dancing flames so that it seemed that the very sky was burning.

'Put that shitting light out!' a hoarse voice called angrily from the parade ground below. 'Or I'll put a shitting round through yer window!'

Miserably Stuermer let the curtain fall back into place and returned to his chair. 'I care little for the Führer's new offensive in Russia. I am attempting to save the Ploesti oil, not so that he can launch that attack. I am prepared to take any and every risk to stop those American bombers destroying Ploesti, because if there are no more supplies of aviation fuel for our fighters, the Americans and the

English bombers will slaughter us, Greul. They will turn *all* our cities into the same sort of stone desert which Berlin has become. The Anglo-Americans are hesitant enough about a great blood-letting in Europe when they invade. Why, therefore, shouldn't they bring Germany to its knees by bombing . . . bombing . . . bombing . . . until finally our poor people have had enough and will plead for peace? Without the Ploesti oil, the home front is condemned to collapse sooner or later.' Abruptly his voice hardened, became almost harsh, and he flashed his companion a bitter, savage look. 'There is no other way, Greul. We must make the attempt, cost what it may. *We must!*' Sadly Greul nodded his head in agreement, for once his National Socialist fervour completely vanished. 'You do realize, sir, that you are condemning Stormtroop Edelweiss to death, don't you,' he said conversationally, as if he might have been talking about the weather.

Stuermer nodded, but said nothing.

Greul looked at his sombre face and said, 'Do you think I could have that drink now, sir, please?'

Silently Stuermer agreed and the two officers slumped there in their chairs, nursing their drinks, while outside the sirens of the ambulances shrilled as they brought their fresh freights of human misery out to the suburban hospitals.

SIX

Lieutenant von Ernst frowned through the jagged shell-hole in the side of his 'nest' – a wrecked Sherman tank, filled with bundles of rags to make the metal floor a little comfortable, the skeleton of a long dead tank commander still poised carefully in the shattered turret above to keep off American souvenir hunters.

Outside, the desert was littered with similar wrecks: half-trucks, tanks, armoured cars either ripped open, burned black or turned a red rust by the salt-laden sea breeze. All victims of the two years of battle which had been fought back and forth along the coastal road since 1940.

Most of them still contained the grim souvenirs of what happened when a solid armour-piercing shell, travelling at 5,000 kilometres an hour, struck a tank: it would churn around inside, rend the crew into shamble-fragments like the pile of choppings thrown out by the butcher for the scavenging dogs. Now that pulverized mass of flesh had turned into fragments of skeletal bone, as the unknown Tommy tank commander who guarded the entrance to von Ernst's 'nest' had. But the lone fugitive from the defeated *Afrika Korps* was glad of the gory artefacts of battle. Even the desert Arabs, the world's most proficient looters, kept away from them. It was just the kind of cover a 'sleeper' needed.

It was a week now since he had killed the survivor of the seaplane crew. The Americans had found him first, dragging the poor wounded wreck back to their camp, cheering and jeering, leading him in with a rope around his neck, as if he were some kind of wild animal. They had begun grilling him at once, led by a big bull of a captain with the gleaming metal wings of a pilot on his broad chest, pushing the wounded airman back and forth from one American to another, till finally unable to stand any more he had sunk to the sand, tears streaming down his ashen young face.

Von Ernst had been too far away to hear what was being said, but he could see from the look on the big Captain's face and the angry glances the others flung at the prisoner that the lone German was still not prepared to talk.

It was then that the Captain had ordered one of the others to bring one of the piss buckets from a tent nearby. To cries of approval and derision from the others, he had poured the evil-smelling contents over the prisoner's upturned face and then rammed the bucket firmly over the man's head. A broom had been brought. The Captain had seized it in his massive paws and then with a great swing, his muscles bulging brutally through the tight material of his shirt, he had whacked the broom against the metal pail. Even at that distance von Ernst had heard it and winced at the thought of the pain that the torturers were inflicting on their poor victim.

The pail had been removed and the prisoner had almost fallen to the sand. Blood streamed from his nostrils and ears, and his terrified face had been as white as chalk. The big bull of a Captain had reached down and grabbed the prisoner by his long hair, pulling him close to his own brutal face. Again, he had rapped out a question, and the lone watcher had guessed what it was. 'Why are you here?'

Their prisoner had been unable to speak. He had bitten his bottom lip until the blood had begun to trickle down his chin. The American had cried out with rage, and grabbing the pail he had dumped it on the German's head once more before seizing the broom.

Von Ernst had swallowed hard at the thought of what he would have to do now. He felt no rancour at the Americans down below torturing his fellow countryman. The war and the desert had brutalized them, like it brutalized every soldier in the end, whatever his nationality. Soon, they knew they, too, would die. What did one more death matter? Yet, to have to kill another German in cold-blood – von Ernst was unable to think that particular horrifying thought through to the end. Yet he knew it had to be done. Sooner or later, the prisoner would speak, and the German mission – whatever it was – would be lost. With hands that trembled slightly, he started to take the parts of his collapsible sniper's rifle from beneath his dirty gown. Not daring to think about it, he commenced fitting it together while from below came the terrible systematic whack of the broom against the piss bucket. He fitted the sniper-scope and brought the rifle up.

The face of the big bull of an American wielding the broom had loomed large in the gleaming calibrated circle of glass. Its every feature had been outlined, the broad nose with the tuft of black hairs sticking out of the nostrils, the thick bushy eyebrows and the determined cleft jaw. For one long instant, von Ernst's finger had taken first pressure and he had been tempted to blast that confident American face into a bloody mess. But he had restrained himself – just in time.

Again the Americans had whipped the bucket from their victim's head to reveal a puffed-up, blackened monstrosity, from whose ears and nose blood jetted. Von Ernst had bitten his bottom lip, as he stared at that terrible, unrecognizable face through his sniper's scope. Then he had swallowed hard and done what he had to.

The crack of the single bullet and the thud of the rifle against his skinny shoulder had surprised him. Down below, as if seen by slow motion, the victim had thrown up his arms, the front of his ragged shirt suddenly staining a bright red – a stain which grew and grew, as he sank to the sand, while all around him the Americans stared open-mouthed and gaping like a collection of village yokels.

Abruptly, the big bull of a pilot had dropped his broom, and flung his paw in the direction of von Ernst's hiding place. In an instant, von Ernst snapped out of his reverie and, suddenly awake to his own danger, rifle still in hand, had run for it – zig-zagging through the dunes, his wounded leg forgotten as he fled for his life . . .

That had been a week ago. Day after day they had searched for him, their trucks and jeeps, laden with armed MPs, had combed the whole area, reaching far out into the desert; he had observed their dust trails from morning to night. Twice they had ventured into this tank graveyard near the coastal road, but even the hard-bitten MPs with their gleaming white helmets and sun-glasses hadn't had the nerve to examine these gory souvenirs of the desert battles. Their search had been perfunctory and on the second and final occasion he had heard one of them call to the NCO in charge, 'Jez-us, Sarge, just let's get the hell outa this place! It gives me the heebie-jeebies! Do ya know there's a guy in there – without a goddam head?' That afternoon, von Ernst had touched the skeletal leg of the dead man above him in the turret, its skinny white bone mocked by the sturdy black boot in which it was still encased, and had breathed gratefully, 'Well, Percy (this was the name he had given to the guardian of the 'nest'), you did it again, old boy. I'll give you a decent burial one of these days for that.'

All the same, in spite of the fact that the Americans had apparently called off the search, he had been unable to send any messages. For some reason they had grounded all aircraft so, he reasoned, there would be no radio traffic passing back and forth between the field and the Liberators, meaning a transmission from him would be easily located.

Now, for the first time since the seaplane had been wrecked, their planes were flying again, the great silver birds zooming in at a hundred or less metres to drop their practice bombs in the circles formed by the engineers pissing on the sand of the desert. He knew it would be safe to transmit again.

He took his eyes off the scene outside and turned his attention to his sleeper's radio, a neat little set in a smart brown case, weighing less than 12 kilos, but which was capable of reaching tremendous distances. He frowned. If only he could receive, he would know what Berlin wanted. Why had they sent that lone seaplane? Like most lonely men von Ernst spoke aloud to himself on such occasions, although he knew well he might be overheard by some passing Arab or American; but he knew, too, if he didn't talk aloud to give the impression of not being alone, he would go mad sooner or later. What did Berlin want to know?

Slowly he started to undo the catches. While he did so, he began to formulate his message for Berlin so that he would be on the air for the shortest possible time; for he knew that gave any enemy detector unit less change of homing in on his transmitter. 'What am I going to say? . . . Americans stepping up bombing practice . . . Right . . . Now what else? . . . Is there anything particularly significant about the trial bombing runs?'

Von Ernst scratched his side. He was already quite lousy from the lack of washing – he had to ration the water he had cached in the 'nest' carefully. One night soon he must sneak down to the beach and bathe in the sea to get rid of the tics and the lice.

Just at that moment another flight of Liberators thundered in, so low that he had to hold his hands over his ears to block out the tremendous roar. They flashed by the wrecked tank sending it shuddering from side to side as if struck by a sudden tempest. Above him Percy trembled audibly. And then they were gone, diving to their target.

Von Ernst took his hands from his ears and clicked his thumb and forefinger together. 'Of course, the way they're flying these practice runs at such a low level!' He flashed a look through the jagged shell-hole in the side of the nest just in time to catch the silver birds roaring high into the bright hard blue of the sky, trailing streams of brown smoke behind them. 'They weren't much higher than fifty metres,' he said to himself. 'I must tell Berlin that. It could be important.'

Expertly he attached the collapsible aerial of the sleeper

transmitter to that of the Sherman and began to send, unaware that his observation that the Liberators were flying their practice bomber runs at such low levels would decide the fate of 286 US heavy bombers and that of 2,829 American airmen – killed or captured . . .

SEVEN

'STILLGESTANDEN!'

The command thundered back and forth over the multiple loudspeakers across the wind-swept airfield. As one, eighty pairs of mountain boots clashed to attention.

Ox-Jo moaned weakly. 'Holy strawsack, it's like a barrage of shitting eighty-eights! Oh, my poor old nut.' Gently, he raised his hand to his forehead, where a coloured handkerchief soaked in vinegar protruded from below the rimless paratroop helmet he wore. 'Why did I do it, oh why?'

Standing to attention next to him in the front of Stormtroop Edelweiss, his yellow face damp with sweat in the hot July sunshine, Jap sneered. 'I'll tell you why. 'Cos you've gotta little bird in that big wooden head of yourn which goes twit-twit. 'Cos yer *meschugge*.'

'Well, a feller likes to have the odd bowl of suds every now and again,' Ox-Jo moaned, as the gleaming, white, twin-engined plane touched down for a perfect three-point landing and began to roll towards the line of Junkers 52's.

'The odd bowl! God in heaven, you had a shitting bath-tub full! And then those poxed-up pavement pounders. I mean a normal bloke takes one of that kind to bed with him, perhaps even two if he's feeling a bit randy. But I've never heard of anybody taking *three* bits of gash into the hay with him! That's downright greedy, you deserve everything you get, Ox. I shouldn't be surprised if your thing doesn't fall off in yer hand one of these days soon.'

'Don't say things like that. I was pissing five different ways already this morning,' Ox-Jo protested with sudden alarm, as the white plane rolled to a stop and the door began to open. With a very shaky hand he reached into his back pocket and brought out a pair of startlingly red silk knickers. Hastily, he mopped his damp brow with them, as the band struck up *das Deutschlandlied.*[1]

An immensely fat figure appeared at the exit of the plane, as the brass boomed to an end, and stood there gazing reflectively at the parade drawn up for his inspection. Even though the troopers were stood to attention, they could not repress their gasps of astonishment at that strange apparition. Even Major Greul's mouth dropped open stupidly.

Goering was dressed in what appeared to be a Roman senator's toga, complete with sandals and laurel crown. At his side hung an ancient sword, its hilt and scabbard, heavily encrusted with precious stones, glittering in the rays of the sun.

'Great crap on the Christmas Tree,' Jap croaked hoarsely, 'he's even got his shitting toe nails painted!'

With a great beam on his berouged fat face, *Reichsmarschall* Goering, Air Force Minister, Head of State of Prussia, Chief of the German Parliament, Commander of the Brownshirts, Chief State Forester and Head of German Station Mission to Fallen Girls, waddled to the waiting Stormtroop Edelweiss.

Graciously he accepted Colonel Stuermer's immaculate salute, raising his beringed finger in the Roman salute by way of reply, and then ushered by the tall mountaineer-colonel puffed his way up and down the ranks of the soldiers standing rigidly to attention, pausing every now and again to stare with a professional eye at the collection of medals most of the veterans bore on their skinny chests.

He stopped in front of Ox-Jo, wheezing for breath, and stared up at the NCO's imposing figure; then his doped gaze fell on the medals in gold, white and black enamel that covered his tight-fitting tunic. As a connoisseur of such things, Goering gave a soft whistle of admiration at the sight of Ox-Jo's collection. '*Alle achtung, Spiess*[2] you've

[1] The German National Anthem.
[2] Roughly, 'Very admirable, Sarn't-Major'.

got a fine collection of tin there.[1] You've even cured your throat-ache, I see,' he indicated the Knight's Cross of the Iron Cross which hung around Ox-Jo's bull-like neck. 'A rare decoration for a non-commissioned officer.'

Ox-Jo looked down at the fat monstrosity who had once proudly called himself 'Germany's Man-of-Destiny' and decided that he looked like some over-fed warm brother, the kind that picked up skinny, painted kids behind Berlin's main station. He could hardly restrain his disgust as he replied, 'Won for Folk, Fatherland and Führer, *Herr Reichsmarschall*.'

Irony was wasted on Hermann Goering. 'Excellent, excellent, Sarn't-Major,' he exclaimed enthusiastically, 'just the kind of sentiment I expected from Stormtroop Edelweiss. Here, wait one moment.' While Stuermer and Greul frowned and Ox-Jo stared down at the fat politician in amazement, Goering fumbled with the leather pouch which dangled down the front of his toga and produced a handful of gleaming gold coins. 'Here,' he said, thrusting them into Ox-Jo's hand, 'French Louis d'Or, legitimate booty of war. Buy yourself some suds with it.' And with that Hermann Goering passed onto the raised platform at the far end of the parade-ground, leaving Ox-Jo to stare at his fat back in astonishment.

'Sweet weeping Jesus!' Jap exclaimed gazing open-mouthed at the fist-full of coins in Ox-Jo's big paw. 'Buy yersen some suds with it, he sez. Oh my aching back, you could buy yersen a whole shitting brewery with that kind of marie!'

'Soldiers of Stormtroop Edelweiss, *comrades*!' Goering's hoarse guttural voice, magnified a dozen times by the microphones, thundered across the square, sending the rooks nesting in the old oaks at the far end flapping into the blue sky, cawing in angry protest. 'I have come personally this day to speed you on your way, because I value you and your devotion to the cause of our German Fatherland, and because I am very conscious of the vital

[1] Slang name for medals.

importance of your mission far away from your homeland in the burning wastes of Africa.'

'Shit on the shingle!' Jap snarled out of the side of his mouth, 'he'll have me crying in me beer next. Burning wastes of Africa – my arse!'

'We Germans are at this moment involved in a grave crisis, a very grave crisis indeed. The Western Allies with their air gangsters are doing serious damage to our cities in the homeland. In the south the Anglo-Americans prepare to invade the continent of Europe and in Russia our glorious *Wehrmacht* faces stubborn and serious resistance from the Bolshevik hordes. In the face of such a serious situation there are some among us who waver, who maintain, even, that there is no hope for Germany.' Goering wagged a finger like a small pork sausage in front of his fat moon-like face. 'I hold no truck with such weak Willies and defeatists. Germany will survive, nay, not just survive, it will overcome and conquer and ensure that this Empire created by our beloved Führer, Adolf Hitler, will endure another thousand years as he has promised us . . .'

Stuermer let the words drone on, full of the professional rhetoric of the trained orator, heavy with grandiloquent phrases that meant nothing. He let his eyes wander around the parade ground, taking it in, knowing that within the hour they would have flown away, perhaps never to return to their homeland again. He thought, with a sudden passionate longing, of those remote mountains in the Himalayas; that white gleaming defiant peak of the 'German Mountain', *Nanga Parbat*, which he had dreamed of conquering ever since he had seen it emerge from the Himalayan mist, so long ago. How good it would be to be there now, away from the cheap brown-shirted, black-booted cruel vulgarity of this vaunted '1,000 Reich', as Hitler called his empire – conquered at the price of hundreds of thousands of dead young soldiers.

But, snapping out of his reverie as Goering ranted on, Stuermer knew that was not to be. His fate had been decided for him.

'We must hold on, hold on and continue to hold on!' Goering was saying, his face flushed a deep purple by now, banging down his pudgy fist on the rostrum in front of him. 'That is all. Hold on another summer and then, comrades, you will see the change that takes place in the affairs of the world.' He gave a mocking laugh. 'This winter that fat sot Winston Churchill and his crippled Jew of a running-mate Franklin Delano Roosevelt will laugh on the other side of their treacherous faces. For the Führer will loose his new secret weapons upon them. Yes, our revenge will be terrible for their terror attacks on our innocent women, old men and children. That red scum, Stalin, will receive his due punishment, too, comrades, when our panzer divisions sweep to the attack once more. I dare say, he'll show us a clean pair of heels this autumn. But, comrades,' Goering raised his finger in warning, 'we must hold on and in your case, you must ensure that our supplies of oil are not stopped. Remember, the eyes of the whole of Germany are upon you, and that you take the best wishes of our own beloved Leader with you. Only this very morning I spoke with him of your mission – after I informed him that our sleeper in North Africa has signalled us that the Americans are stepping up their preparations for a low-level raid on Ploesti – and he replied to me, "My dear Goering, please tell your good fellows that I am with them heart and soul. We will be ready for the US air pirates when they come. But it is our wish that they should be destroyed long before it comes to that." ' Goering's drugged gaze swept over the ranks of soldiers standing rigidly to attention, the sweat now pouring down their tough bronzed faces. 'The Führer's last words to me for you were these,' He raised his voice. ' "I, your Leader, command you, of Stormtroop Edelweiss, to seek out the Americans and destroy them and their machines of death – *every last one of them*! Be ruthless and remorseless. Germany's fate lies in your hands!" '

Goering's voice trailed away, and the energy drained from him as if someone had suddenly opened a tap.

Stuermer, watching him from below, as his last words echoed and re-echoed metallically, saw again, as he had that first time, that Goering was at the end of his tether. He was a broken man, living on his nerves, his drugs and the fanciful illusions of his kind. Perhaps all these golden pheasants[1] were.

All the same, Goering's last words sent an odd chill down his spine. *'Germany's fate lies in your hands!'* God, were things as bad as that?

Abruptly, the tall drum major brought down his mace. The band blared into noisy, brassy life. Stuermer recalled his military duties. He licked his lips. 'Stormtroop Edelweiss,' he bellowed above the music, 'Stormtroop Edelweiss – *shoulder arms*!'

As one, the eighty troopers slammed their rifles through the three separate movements of the 'shoulder arms', each movement punctuated by the hard slap of palms against wood. Mentally Stuermer counted off the seconds and then ordered, 'Stormtroop Edelweiss – will advance . . . *PARADE MARCH!'*

Shoulders thrown back, eyes fixed woodenly on some distant object, legs moving waist-height, the mountaineers advanced like automatons to the tune of the 'Prussian Parade March', all heavy drumbeat and shrill brass.

'Eyes . . . *eyes right!*' Stuermer commanded as they came level with Goering on his rostrum, bringing up his own right hand smartly to touch his cap in salute.

Weakly Goering raised his arm in the 'German greeting'[2] swaying visibly as he did so and supporting the upraised arm with his other hand, as if it were unutterably heavy. And then they were past and to their front the propellers of the old-fashioned Junkers – 'Aunt Jus', the troops called them – started to revolve, as they prepared to take their soldier passengers to the field where the gliders were waiting for them.

Mechanically Colonel Stuermer and his mountaineers

[1] Slang name for Nazi Party officials.
[2] The Nazi salute.

marched towards them, each man knowing that the die was cast and there was no turning back. They were on their way . . .

And over three thousand kilometres away, another group of bold, young men in a different uniform, marching to the sounds of a Souza march, filed by Killer Kane standing high on a rostrum not unlike the one on which Goering now sagged. They were not as smart, perhaps, as Storm-troop Edelweiss, but they were just as determined; for they, too, had just heard that their fate was sealed – from the lips of Colonel Kane. The secret was out! On the morning of Sunday, August 1st, 1943 they would fly the great attack mission on Ploesti. There were fourteen short days to go before the raid that would cripple the German war machine.

Out of Kane's sight, Bull Bulcombe nudged the chaplain Father Beck who marched at his side and said, 'Well, sky-pilot, what do you say? You got good connections up there?' He indicated the burning, blue desert sky.

Father Beck, white-haired, jovial and sunburnt, grinned and said, 'Sure, son. I pray through channels though.' Now it was Bull's turn to grin. 'Well get those channels working, padre, and make contact for us with your boss. We're gonna need all the help we can get.'

Behind them Shorty Perkins shook his head in mock disbelief and said a quick 'Hail Mary'. This was no time, he told himself, to make jokes about God . . .

The actors were in place; the drama could begin.

BOOK TWO

'Silent cannons, soon to cease your silence
Soon unlimber'd to begin the red business.'

Whitman, 'Drum Taps', 1865

ONE

'WHOMP . . . WHOMP . . . WHOMP . . .'

Hastily, the mountaineers of Stormtroop Edelweiss grabbed for holds, as the big Dornier glider swung to the left alarmingly.

Ox-Jo opened his eyes and said in bewilderment, staring around at the suddenly ashen faces of the troopers, 'Did somebody knock?'

'Of course, they did, you stupid currant-crapper!' Jap snorted, hanging on for dear life, as the glider heeled to the right, while the pilot tensed, sweating over the controls, his face coloured a scarlet-red hue by the flames from below. 'There's only a Tommy cruiser down there, shooting every shitting pop-gun he has at us, and may I remind you, Sergeant, crapping Major, crapping Meir, that this crate is made of wood, canvas and brown wrapping-paper.'

'Oh, is that all,' Ox-Jo said cheerfully as the glider dropped a sheer fifty metres as another salvo of 37mm shells exploded directly below it. 'Nothing serious then, eh? I can hit the hay again, can't I? You see, I've just got Zarah Leander[1] on her back with her legs in the air, and anything can happen now – and probably will—'

He broke off suddenly, as in the pilot's cockpit an alarm bell started to shrill and lights flashed off and on alarmingly.

'Oh, I'll piss in my boot,' Jap exclaimed fearfully. 'Now the clock's struck thirteen. We're gonna go down in the drink.'

Stuermer raised his voice above the sudden burst of scared chatter in the big glider and the thunder of the anti-aircraft barrage from the British ships down below in the Mediterranean. 'There's no need for panic,' he com-

[1] Famous German movie star of the period.

manded. 'It's just the towing plane signalling to us . . . Everyone be perfectly calm. There's a cloud bank ahead. We'll be out of sight in a few moments.'

Stuermer wiped the beads of gleaming sweat from his own forehead, and stared down through the perspex at the tiny grey ships far below, their red lights winking as they blasted away at the aircraft flying overhead; then he forgot the Royal Navy and turned to Witzig, the glider pilot, who fought the controls as the light canvas and wood plane was buffeted back and forth by the shells exploding all around in ugly bursts of brown smoke. 'Can you make it, Witzig?' he asked in a low voice.

Witzig, the veteran, forced his strained damp face into a tight smile. 'The urine's trickling down my left leg I must admit,' he said grimly, not taking his eyes off the cloud bank to their front for which the Junkers 52 was heading at a steady 150 kilometres an hour, 'but I think we'll survive—'

A shell exploded right to their front, and the nose of the Dornier was blasted into the air like a wild horse bucking angrily. Stuermer reeled against the side of the cockpit and gasped, '*Himmel Herr Gott*! . . . Can't that Auntie Ju get a move on? They'll have us if we don't hit that cloud soon!'

Tracer shells streamed towards them in a lethal white rain. For a moment he and the pilot were blinded. Then they were through and the damp white cloud embraced them like a protective mother a frightened child.

Stuermer breathed out hard and wiped the sweat from his forehead with his handkerchief. At his side, Witzig freed himself and wiped each damp hand in turn on the knee of his grey coveralls. 'It could have been worse, *Herr Oberst*,' he said.

'But not much.'

'No, you're right there sir,' Witzig answered as Stuermer flung a hasty glance backwards at his ashen-faced troopers. Nobody had been hit. They had come through the enemy naval barrage unscathed, but Stuermer knew that the cruiser down below would be at this very minute radioing the shore-based enemy fighters of the presence of the German planes in this area of airspace. It wouldn't be long before the Hurricanes and Spitfires would be on their way to intercept them. 'What's the drill now, Witzig?' he asked, as to the rear, the troopers lined up to vomit in the already overflowing piss bucket towards the end of the fuselage.

'Well, *Herr Oberst*, my guess is that we're about sixty kilometres away from the North African coast now,' the glider pilot replied, his gaze fixed intently on the dripping wet metal cable that linked them to the Junkers 52. 'I should expect we'll soon be casting off. With a bit of luck it'll be dark by the time we start crossing the coast itself and that should help us—' He broke off, suddenly. A red light was winking on the control panel in front of him. 'Speak of the devil,' he grunted, eyes flashing from one point to the other, as he prepared for what would happen next. 'They're going to release us. Hold on, Colonel!'

Witzig gripped the steering column firmly in both his big capable hands, jaw clenched, shoulder muscles ready to take the strain as soon as the towing cable fell away. 'Here we go,' he cried in the same instant that the tow fell from sight and the glider shuddered violently, a strange almost eerie silence descending upon the canvas and wood structure.

Witzig brought up the nose. The glider answered immediately sailing up high through the clouds and losing the Junkers 52 at once.

They were alone in the bank of wet clouds, moving forward in utter silence, trailing a mighty black shadow behind them. For a few moments Stuermer was intrigued by the sensation. Everything seemed so peaceful. He felt he could open the door, step out onto the clouds, and saunter across the billowing white surface. But the sound of Ox-Jo's Bavarian accent growling, 'Heaven, arse and twine, now we're flying on wound elastic bands!' awoke him to reality once more. 'Can you see the other plane, Witzig?' he asked swiftly, craning his neck forward in an attempt to spot the second glider carrying the other half of Stormtroop Edelweiss.

Witzig, all his energy directed to keeping the glider on course and not lose height – for he would need every metre of altitude he could gain for the long powerless flight in front of him – shook his head.

'No sir, but don't worry. Captain Hermeskeil is one of the best glider pilots in the whole of Germany. Indeed,' he grinned at Stuermer, the beads of sweat streaming down his skinny face once again with the strain, 'I can think of only one pilot better than he.'

'He couldn't be a certain Lieutenant Hans Witzig, could he?' Stuermer queried, returning his grin.

Witzig winked and said, 'Modesty forbids me to comment on the matter any further, sir.'

The minutes passed leadenly, as the mountaineers came one by one to the cockpit to stare numbly at the bank of wet cloud that barred their way, all of them obviously affected by the strange silence. When it was Ox-Jo's turn, he shuddered dramatically and said, 'Aach, a shitting great louse just ran across my liver, sir! It gives yer the creeps, don't it, sir, up here at three thousand metres in a crate made of glue and paper, with no shitting engine to keep yer flying.'

Stuermer forced a grin. 'You have the gift, you big rogue, of inspiring your fellow men. Glue and paper, indeed! Go on, be off with you, back to your seat!'

Now the clouds started to thin out and the men crouching anxiously in the cockpit could catch occasional glances of the darkening velvet sky beyond through the gaps in the fleecy wasteland to their front. Stuermer screwed up his eyes. Still no sign of the other glider. His apprehension and sense that something had gone wrong began to grow.

And then they were through completely. Below them there were the brilliant white combs of the breakers raking the beach of Africa, and beyond was the vast yellow stretch of the desert, with the night already sweeping across it in a great race of stark black. He craned his head to right and left.

The darkening velvet sky was empty. There was no sign of the other glider. He sucked his teeth and looked down at Witzig. The other nodded grimly. 'Nothing, *Herr Oberst*,' he agreed. 'Nairy a sign of 'em.'

'What do you think, Witzig?'

Witzig hesitated momentarily. 'There are several possibilities. Something went wrong with the tow cast-off. It sometimes happens, though not very often. The Junkers couldn't break the tow, so that would mean your men are on their way back to Sicily. The other possibility is that Hermeskeil has lost his way in the clouds, but I personally think that is hardly likely. Hermeskeil is really a very skilled, expert pilot who knows what he is doing. Then—'

'Go on,' Stuermer prompted when Witzig didn't speak. 'Spit it out. Straight from the shoulder, Lieutenant.'

'Hm, well, sir, that somehow or other Hermeskeil lost control and the glider went down—' Witzig didn't complete the sentence. Instead, he jerked one thumb downwards to the darkening sea.

'Into the drink?' Stuermer gasped.

Witzig nodded.

'*Ach du grosser Gott!*' Stuermer exclaimed and then recovering himself swiftly asked, 'and what kind of a chance do they have if they do go down into the sea?'

Witzig frowned. 'Not so good, sir. The glider would float for a little while admittedly, but, as you can see, they are not exactly robust and besides the exits are very tight. It's normal procedure during an attack landing for the paras to slit open the canvas of the fuselage and go out that way instead of through the door. So,' he shrugged and left the rest of his sentence unfinished.

'They wouldn't have much of a chance,' Stuermer whispered sadly, thinking of the possibility of all those brave young men down there in the sea, choking to death at this very minute.

'Yes, that's about it, Colonel.'

Ten minutes later, just as night fell completely over the desert, Witzig broke the heavy silence that had descended upon the mountaineers after the discovery that the other glider was missing, with, 'Look – to port, Colonel. Your target. You can just see it.'

Hastily Stuermer focused his binoculars.

Just barely visible in the rapidly glowing gloom he could make out the fat-bellied, silver shapes of many bombers parked close together. 'Give me a kilometre reading now,' he snapped over his shoulder, 'and then when we see the last one, another reading.'

'Yes sir,' Witzig answered, promptly taking advantage of a sudden thermal, to raise a little higher and then, losing height, banking slightly to port, while Stuermer swept the huge field with his glasses, just able to make out a tented camp grouped around what appeared to be a permanent building.

Then they were past and Witzig sang out,'Exactly eight kilometres, sir.'

Stuermer did a rapid calculation. 'My God,' he said after a moment,' there's at least one hundred of the monsters on that one field alone!'

'And you've got exactly three officers, including me,' Witzig said in a small voice, suddenly very sobered by the thought, 'and forty soldiers to knock out *that* lot!'

'Exactly,' Stuermer said and slumped back in his seat, suddenly worried . . .

At dawn, the glider started to descend through pearly-white cumulus. The troopers within, shivering in their thin desert uniforms, were clawing open the waxed paper boxes containing their breakfast rations, with stiff fingers, munching the hard black bread and taking bites at the horsemeat salami in silence, as if each man had suddenly realized just how hazardous this mission was that they had undertaken so far away from the Homeland.

Up front with the pilot, Stuermer watched the dripping white cotton-wool clouds begin to part and then, with dramatic suddenness, the sun was there, hanging on the yellow lip of the desert, tingeing the dunes a glowing warm hue. He blinked several times to accustom his eyes to the abrupt light and saw a slow plodding line of camels like some scene from the Bible. 'I'm surprised, Witzig,' he said between bites of a slab of bitter *Luftwaffe* ration chocolate which made up his breakfast, 'I would have thought that we would have left the inhabited area behind us by now.'

Witzig, busy levelling out and taking advantage of the heat thermals that he was now encountering, shook his head. 'We've still got a couple of hundred kilometres to go, sir, before we reach those sand hills – if they exist – and according to my briefing, there'll be Arabs, nomadic Senussi to be exact, for another few kilometres or so before the oases give out.'

Stuermer shot the pilot a look. His taut, young face and bloodshot eyes clearly revealed the strain of the long flight across the Mediterranean and the three or four hundred kilometres he had glided since the towing plane had departed. 'Can you make it, Witzig?' he asked with some concern, for unlike himself and the others Witzig had now been without sleep for twenty-four hours.

'Sure, sir,' Witzig said with forced confidence. 'But, frankly, I'm bursting for a piss. My tonsils are floating in the stuff. Would it be too much to ask a senior German officer to bring the piss bucket forward for a moment?' He grinned.

Stuermer returned the grin. 'For this once, it wouldn't be, Witzig, you rogue.'

One hour later, Witzig began his descent. Greul and Stuermer crouched at his side, surveying the burning yellow desert with their glasses, anxiously on the lookout for any sign of life.

Visibility, in spite of the shimmering heat waves, was amazingly good and at this height they could probably see as far as fifty kilometres. Yet in the whole vast arena of burning sand there was absolutely no sign of life, not a single date palm, not even a patch of parched camel scrub. The whole desert below was empty.

Suddenly, Greul nudged him, glasses held to his eyes. 'Ten o'clock, sir, left of those larger dunes.'

'What is it?' Stuermer asked, swinging his glasses in the same direction.

'Looks like hills, sir.'

A dark smudge, standing out against the yellow wash of sand, loomed up in the gleaming circles of glass. 'The hills our patrols spotted,' he exclaimed.

'Could well be, sir,' Greul agreed. 'They certainly do seem higher than the surrounding terrain.'

Swiftly Stuermer passed on instructions to Witzig, who swung the big machine round in a silently graceful curve, while Stuermer went back briefly into the stiflingly hot fuselage to explain their position to the men.

Another half hour passed. The two observers in the cockpit could now definitely make out a hill feature stretching along the horizon, clear as daylight against the yellow desert floor. The glider started to lose height, racing over the sands, dragging a huge black shadow behind it, as the thermals, which had borne out so well in this tremendous six-hundred-kilometre flight, began to give out.

'How long?' Stuermer queried, lowering his glasses, satisfied now that there was nobody down below.

'About fifteen minutes, I estimate, sir. And won't I be glad to stretch my limbs, at last!'

'You'll get your rest, Lieutenant, I promise you that. Just get us down safely.'

He left Greul to continue the observation and went back to the men who looked at him expectantly, the sweat streaming down their brick-red faces now. 'All right, fifteen minutes to go,' he announced. 'Helmets on!'

Hastily, the men fumbled for their rimless para helmets and placed them on their cropped heads.

Stuermer waited and then continued, 'All right, you know the drill. As soon as I give the word, feet up and duck your heads. Keep your bodies pressed well back and on impact try to keep leaning backwards. All clear?'

'All clear, sir,' Ox-Jo mimicked in a little child's voice. 'Will you just tell me please when the boogeyman has gone so I can open my eyes?'

Stuermer laughed softly. As always the men were in good heart, undeterred by the unknown dangers facing them in this hostile, uncharted desert waste. 'I will . . . All right, prepare for landing!'

The minutes ticked by. The tension inside the glider growing by the instant as the inhospitable ground became ever clearer, revealing, to the alarm of those in the cockpit, that the ridges to their front were not composed of sand. Instead, they seemed to be made of dark, weathered sandstone. And they were alarmingly littered with huge boulders.

Witzig bit his lip. 'I'm running out of air now, gentlemen,' he hissed through clenched teeth. His eyes frantically searched the terrain ahead for a suitable place to land the big glider, with its two thousand kilos of men and material. 'I'll have to put down soon.'

'To port there seems to be a fairly clear run,' Greul snapped. 'Only a few boulders—'

'One's enough, Major,' Witzig cut him short, turning the Dornier to port, as the ground rushed by below them at an ever increasing rate. Using all his strength, Witzig jerked up the nose of the glider, sweat pouring down his tense face in rivulets. 'Help to brake her a bit . . . Come on, you ugly bitch . . . come up . . . *For God's sake, come up!*' he shouted angrily, his every muscle writhing through the sweat-blackened back of his khaki shirt.

Without turning, his gaze fixed hypnotically on the ground racing up to meet them, he yelled, 'Alert your men, Colonel!'

Stuermer spun round. And with the sound of the wind in the Dornier's great wings deafening him, he commanded: 'Ready to land! Raise feet!' Swiftly the mountaineers, all of them pale and anxious, raised their boots and huddled down.

Stuermer grasped a strut; Greul did the same. They were only metres above the surface of the desert now, hurtling ever downwards at over one hundred kilometres an hour. Suddenly, Witzig applied the air brakes. They gave a great alarming screech. A huge boulder loomed up frighteningly. Witzig swung the controls to the right. They missed it by less than a metre. Greul gasped with relief. Before them lay perhaps two hundred metres of downward-sloping desert. Witzig made his decision. 'This is it!' he yelled above the racket of the air brakes. 'God knows what's at the end of that slope! But I can't keep the bitch airborne any longer. *HERE WE GO!*'

Witzig jerked the controls. The Dornier hit the desert. There was the high-pitched shriek of wood and canvas being subjected to unbearable strain. The Dornier bounced high in the air once more, momentarily, the view from the cockpit was obscured by a huge cloud of yellow dust. The glider hit the ground again. The thick barbed-wire, wrapped around the skids to act as an additional brake, started to snap like twine. Rips and tears appeared in the fuselage everywhere in grinding, rending confusion. The glider slithered across the desert, swaying and shuddering frighteningly. The port wing struck a boulder. It splintered like matchwood. Witzig fought valiantly to hold the stricken Dornier on course. To no avail. It started to skid to port. Men tumbled to the floor in a frightened, shouting heap. Equipment broke loose. One of the captured mini motorbikes lurched forward and disappeared through a rent in the canvas. A moment later two mountaineers, fighting desperately to hold on, followed, shrieking with hysterical fear as they did so.

'Look out!' Stuermer yelled in sudden alarm. 'We're going over!'

His cry of alarm was drowned by the deafening grating sound, as Witzig forced the crippled glider round, his eyes wide with fear as the precipice or whatever it was loomed ever larger, with the plane heading straight for it – and final destruction.

Stuermer, his face ashen, the sweat pouring down his body, willed the plane round, his hands clenched in fists, his nails digging cruelly into the palms, desperately praying Witzig would succeed before it was too late. *Fifty metres . . . forty . . . thirty-five metres ... twenty . . . fifteen* . . . There seemed no hope for them now. They were almost over. The stricken glider slithered closer and closer to the edge of that awesome precipice . . . *Ten metres* . . . Like a small child, afraid of the dark, Stuermer closed his eyes and waited for the end. *Five metres* . . .

Suddenly, there was no sound. Only the groans of the bruised, injured mountaineers in the crazy confusion of the fuselage. Their hectic progress across the desert had come to an end! Almost reluctantly, Stuermer opened his eyes. The nose of the glider rested squarely on the edge of a great drop that fell some five hundred metres to the valley below. They had been saved at the very last instant! He wiped the thick sweat from his brow with a hand that trembled slightly. 'God in heaven, Witzig,' he said weakly, 'you deserve a whole cupboard full of medals for—' He stopped short, a gasp of horror on his lips.

Witzig lay pressed back against his canvas and leather seat, his face set in a grimace of absolutely unbearable pain, for the metal steering column had thrust right through his body, pinning him to the seat. Lieutenant Horst Witzig, the Hero of the Capture of Eben Emael, would never again sail high into the sky to soar silently and effortlessly for hours on end, to break yet another record. Horst Witzig was dead.

Slowly, very slowly, Stuermer bent and gently pressed down the eyelids blocking those sightless eyes for ever. Tragedy had struck Stormtroop Edelweiss once again in a brief twenty-four hours. Would it never cease?

TWO

Stuermer raised his hand to his sweat-soaked cap and, for a moment, the men who had dug the graves assumed the position of attention; then Stuermer nodded and, shouldering their shovels, they began to plod wearily back to where the others grouped around their petrol fires, cooking their first hot meal in forty-eight hours.

Stuermer remained standing there for a while longer staring at the three cairns of stones which marked the spot where Witzig and the two troopers who had fallen out of the glider now rested, and wondered if any other human being would see those solitary graves once they left these uncharted remote hills.

He shivered suddenly at the thought and flung an involuntary glance over his shoulder as if he expected to see – he knew not what – there. But the darkening desert floor below was empty, night slowly beginning to throw its dark cloak across its yellow surface. Within the hour it would be pitch black.

Slowly he, too, followed the diggers to where the men crouched over the flickering petrol stoves, their faces hollowed out to death's heads in the blue fitful flames.

He sat down next to Greul who was squatting with his back to the shattered glider which lay there like a great skeletal bird, with its spars showing everywhere through the ripped canvas. 'Well, Major, what's the situation?' Stuermer asked after a moment, using his cap to wipe the sweat off his face; for it was still very hot, though soon, once night fell, it could well be bitterly cold in these desert hills. 'What is *our* situation?'

Greul had recovered his National Socialist energy and dogmatic fervour, it seemed, for he said eagerly, 'Not bad at all, sir. Apart from cuts and bruises the men are all fit. Our supplies are fully intact, including all the explosives, and both the bikes work, though the frame of one of them is slightly buckled.'

Stuermer nodded his approval, as he watched his men eat their supper silently without the usual off-duty banter and horseplay. The desert was having its effect upon them already, he told himself. The vast eternity of nothing but sand always did; he knew that from past experience. 'Water?' he asked laconically.

'Not one of the jerricans was holed, sir,' Greul replied promptly. 'We have enough for five to seven days at full ration, double that time at half.'

Stuermer thought for a moment. 'Half ration it will be, Greul. I don't want to run the risk of going into an oasis to find water unless it is absolutely essential.'

'I agree, sir. We must be self-contained, and we Germans know how to be hard on ourselves.'

Stuermer ignored the comment and took his eyes off Ox-Jo morosely spooning out the meat from his mess-tin full of stew. 'This is the plan, Greul. We let the men sleep till midnight. That will give them four hours. At the stroke of twelve we will set off, with Meier and that little half-breed friend of his doing the scouting at point on the mini-motorbikes.'

'Good, sir. That will give us the advantage of the cool night air.'

'Exactly.'

'And when the sun comes up?'

'If the two scouts report all is clear to our front, I shall allow the men two hours' rest and then we set off again. At midday we will have a proper rest till the sun goes down once more and then we'll march all night.'

Greul made a quick calculation. 'Assuming we can cover fifty kilometres, on average, each twenty-four hours, we should be close to Benghazi in just over a week.'

Stuermer nodded. 'Agreed, if, that is, we encounter no hostile natives, no enemy spotter plane locates us and our food and water supplies hold out. Yes, my dear Greul, you may assume that, if you wish.'

But as always irony was wasted on Greul. His face lit up at the prospect of the long march through the uncharted sand waste ahead of them and he said enthusiastically, 'We of Stormtroop Edelweiss have never failed yet, sir. The men will rise to the challenge, however bold it may be. We will succeed.'

Stuermer was too weary to be infected by his second-in-command's enthusiasm. Instead, he yawned luxuriously, stretched out both arms and twisted his stiff back. 'Holy strawsack, I could sleep for a thousand years! All right, Greul, get the men bedded down and then turn in yourself.'

'Sentries?'

Stuermer stared at the velvet dusk sky, with the silver spectral shape of the sickle moon already present to the east, and shook his head. 'Why not let them all sleep? I doubt if there is another human being within two hundred kilometres of here.' He shivered with sudden cold. Already the air had a nip in it. 'I'm turning in,' he said wearily, grabbing for his pack to rest his head on and his ground-sheet to cover him. 'Good night, Greul.'

'Good night, sir.'

Colonel Stuermer could not get to sleep. Long after his exhausted men were snoring hard and Greul was muttering incoherently next to him, lost in some bad dream or other, he was still awake. Above him, now, the desert sky was pitted with a myriad stars, harsh and brilliant-silver, and so close that he felt he could have reached up easily and snatched one of them down. And all around him he could hear the old familiar sound – one he remembered well from his pre-war climbing expeditions – of the singing desert sands. For as the millions of sand-grains contracted in the night cold, moving and rubbing against one another, they made a strange haunting music that had something eerie about it.

He thought of the events of the last thirty-six hours and wondered once again what had happened to the other glider and the luckless men aboard it. He prayed that they were safe and smiled at the thought of them back in Sicily, enjoying the unexpected time out of war, celebrating with much *vino* and the compliant, buxom, dark-eyed Sicilian girls. He hoped they were, at least.

On sudden impulse, he crawled out from underneath his ground sheet and pulled on his mountain boots which were stiff with cold. Gingerly, he crept through the little camp, not wishing to disturb his snoring men who lay huddled under their groundsheets like corpses. He dismissed the comparison hurriedly and paused outside the camp to stare out across the glowing desert in the direction they would take at midnight.

He could see for kilometres across that vast dead land, in which nothing lived and nothing grew, harsh, cruel and inhospitable. He frowned abruptly, feeling that somehow the land saw him and his men as intruders. It was an odd sensation and he shuddered, fighting back the feeling that perhaps there was something out there after all, *watching* him; that, as he watched, he was being watched!

'Silly fool,' he grunted to himself. 'You're like a foolish old woman always thinking there are robbers under the bed.' All the same, he turned and hurried back to the security of his fellow soldiers, glad to be in their company once more. Five minutes later he was snoring as soundly as the rest of Stormtroop Edelweiss . . .

Three hours later they were on their way, strung in a long file in the hills, their pace brisk for it was cold, hands dug deep in their pockets for warmth, heads bent into the protection of their collars, while Ox-Jo and Jap putt-putted away to their front on their mini-motorbikes.

The going was easy in spite of the forty-kilo load of personal equipment, weapons, explosives and petrol which each man carried, for the ground underfoot was firm and hard, unlike the shifting loose sand that the Edelweiss troopers had expected to find in the desert. In the lead Stuermer and Greul guided the men simply by following the tracks made by the two motorbike riders, who were scouting ahead on a compass bearing.

Stuermer was beginning to forget the lurking apprehensions of the previous day. The night air was clear and invigorating and there was something soothing now, about the vastness of the star-studded velvet sky above them, as they progressed like a black worm across that immense high plateau. He told himself they were going to succeed. However impossible the mission – a handful of men against all the resources of the mightiest country in the world – Stuermer knew at that moment that Stormtroop Edelweiss would accomplish it. They would! He plodded on happily.

Ox-Jo and Jap, a kilometre or two to the front of the column, had no time for the immensity of the night sky and the chances of success. Their thoughts were concentrated strictly on the terrain and their compasses as they wove in and out of the huge boulders which littered the plateau everywhere, their eyes glued on the green glowing needle of the compasses attached to the handlebars of the tiny chugging bikes, advancing steadily at thirty kilometres an hour.

'Christ, I feel like a shitting monkey on a stick!' Ox-Jo growled, as he hunched his huge bulk over the tiny bike.

'Yer, and yer look like one, too,' Jap answered, neatly swerving by a stretch of rock rubble which blocked his way and yelping as he hit a rock hidden under the sand. 'But it's shitting hard on the arse! My piles are getting piles at this rate.'

'Couldn't happen to a nicer feller,' Ox-Jo guffawed and freeing one hand indicated a narrow chasm formed by two immensely high boulders to their front. 'We'll make a break there, Jap, and have a look-see what's up ahead.'

'Good idea,' Jap answered. 'Give the old *derrière* a rest for a bit. The lads are kilometres behind us now.'

Carefully, the two of them steered their bikes into the chasm, the rocks on both sides momentarily so high that they shut out the silver light of the stars. Then they were through, and braking their bikes on terrain that was all of a sudden soft and treacherous.

Ox-Jo breathed a sigh of relief, as he swung a stiff leg over the hard saddle of the little bike. 'I don't know, Jap, I suppose it's better than walking, but not much.' He walked to the head of the trail, mentally noting the soft, loose sand underfoot, and stared out at the desert below. 'Looks as if we're getting out of the hills, Jap,' he commented moodily.

His running-mate, standing at his side now, nodded. 'Yer, Ox, in a couple of hours when the rest of them reach here, they're gonna start cursing. It'll be a hard slog, the way they're laden. The sand's shitting soft.'

'Too right.' Ox-Jo forgot the sand and, remembering their mission, put up his night glasses and systematically searched the desert from left to right, checking the way ahead for hidden dangers, while Jap, who had the keenest eyesight of all, a legacy of his native father, did the same. Suddenly, both of them hesitated and, re-focusing, excitedly examined what appeared to be a vehicle parked a long way off to their right – but it was no more than a large rock. '*Himmel, Arsch und Wolkenbruch!*' Jap cursed softly. 'Out here in the middle of nowhere, you can imagine all sorts of shitting things. All that sand – it gets right on my tits.'

Ox-Jo nodded and said, 'Don't you talk to me about tits, Jap. It's bin so long ago since I had a bit of the other, that I've plain forgot what a nice big fat milk factory looks like.' He put the night glasses back in the leather case. 'Come on, arse with ears, let's get back to the CO and report.' Together, they started to slog back to where their bikes were, the sand crystals glittering brightly in the hard cruel silver of the stars.

They had almost reached them when Jap started back, as if he had spotted a snake or deadly black desert scorpion in his path. He gave a sudden gasp, yellow wizened face blanched and frightened.

'What is it?' Ox-Jo stopped instinctively and stared at

his companion, who was standing there as if mesmerized, skinny little paw pointing to the ground. 'Well, come on, you little yellow turd, cough it—'

The words died on his lips, as he saw what Jap was pointing at. Clearly defined in the sand, almost parallel to the marks made by their own nailed mountaineer boots, there was a trail of other footprints – those of a naked foot. He swallowed hard. 'Hot shit, Jap. S-s-somebody . . .' He stuttered to a stop, overcome by the realization of what those naked footprints meant.

Slowly, very slowly Jap nodded his head. 'Yer, somebody's out here – *now* . . .'

THREE

Five hundred kilometres further north another lone figure stood, as if frozen thus for eternity, staring in horrified wonder at the thing on the sand: the only sound his own harsh breathing and the slither back and forth of the shingle on the beach below.

Leutnant von Ernst swallowed hard and took a closer look. It was a human leg, bare from the severed gory knee to where the boot started, one of the ankle-high type worn by Germany's *Gebirgsjager*[1].

He licked his suddenly parched lips and examined it a little closer in the bright silver of the stars, forgetting the horror of the sight. He was on the right trail. There was no doubt about that. They had to be here somewhere or other, he knew that now.

He had been searching now ever since he had been first startled inside the 'nest' by the chatter of machine-guns close by and had seen the Ami Lightning fighters snarling around in the bright blue sky, dragging their cotton-white vapour trails behind them, as they tried to shoot down the cloud-jumping, ancient, three-engined plane. It had been easy to recognize it. It was an old Auntie Ju!

But the Ami fighter pilots had been unlucky. The much slower Junkers, with its corrugated metal sides, had been able to avoid each snarling pass easily until finally it had succeeded in dodging into a thick bank of cloud. For a few minutes the Lightnings had persisted in their search, but in the end they had given up. Obviously, they had begun to run out of fuel. In angry frustration they had been forced to form up again and set off back to their base at Dernia.

[1] Mountain troops.

He had been crouching there, wondering what to make of this second German plane to appear off the coast so surprisingly, when a silent camouflaged shape had come scudding out of the clouds and there had been no mistaking the black and white crosses adorning its giant wings. 'A glider,' he had cried to himself, 'a German glider!' Almost before he had absorbed that startling piece of information the great silent Dornier had disappeared beyond the dunes to the west, leaving him there gaping at the burning blue sky in open-mouthed awe. Ten minutes later the ground on which he had crouched had shuddered. There had been a thick throaty crump and far, far away, a thin column of smoke had ascended to the heavens. 'It can only be the glider,' he had told himself and hastily said a prayer for the souls of those unknown Germans out there who might well have perished in the explosion.

All that day he had observed the area to the west from his hideout in the 'nest'. But there had been no sign of the Americans. The whole long afternoon, while he willed it to get dark, the great lumbering Liberators had come zooming out of the sky to practise their low-level runs on the targets below. It seemed, he thought, that the Amis had noted nothing.

As soon as it had begun to grow dark, he had set off, with two extra water bottles slung across his skinny chest, a looted American grease-gun hidden beneath his dirty robe, heading for the spot to the west where he had seen the column of smoke that morning.

For two solid hours he had trekked along the desert road, diving into the drainage ditch at its side every time he had seen the blue lights of the American trucks plying up and down between the fields around Benghazi. He had been just about to give up in despair when he had found the severed foot, lying there on the sand before him, now, so incongruously. Now, he knew he was on the right trail. He set off again with renewed hope, the way ahead clearly outlined by the light of the stars.

Ten minutes later he received new confirmation that he

was on the correct track. Right to his front, he spotted two deep ruts in the sand, ploughing along the beach erratically, heading for the dunes to his front. He recognized them immediately. They were those made by the skids attached to a glider's base. He hurried on the best he could with his wounded leg, gasping a little harshly now with the effort. So concerned was he with finding the missing glider that he almost stumbled blindly over a corpse, partially covered by sand, lying between the ruts made by the skids. He stopped and bent down on one knee.

A tough young face stared up at him, but where the eyes had once been, there were two purple suppurating pits. He gasped with shock. The gulls, the great beach-scavengers, had already paid a visit, picking out the two glittering orbs that had first attracted their attention. When light came again, they would be back for more.

Trying to avoid looking at that ghastly sight, he fumbled with the stiff buttons of the man's tunic and took out his paybook. Tilting the open pages to one side, making the most of the silver light, he read out the list of campaigns that the dead soldier, one Alois Schmuckle, had taken part in – Narvik, Crete, the Battle of the Ice Sea, Caucasus etc., etc. Then, leaning back on his heels, eyes averted from that mutilated face, von Ernst tried to put the various pieces of the jigsaw together.

Alois was a typical Bavarian or Austrian Christian name. Again the dead man wore mountain boots, as had the severed leg, and the campaigns that Schmuckle had taken part in were those which had been fought predominantly by mountain troops.

He frowned and speaking to himself as always, asked, 'But what, in three devils' name, are mountain troops doing out here in the desert?' He leafed through the man's paybook once more, but could find nothing there to explain what these *Gebirgsjager* were doing in Africa – save for a blurred snapshot taken on the peak of a high, snow-covered mountain of a handful of grinning soldiers, laden with packs and equipment, with the words MOUNT ELBRUS[1] written below.

He shrugged. It meant nothing to him. Carefully he tucked away the paybook in his robe, and shouldering his grease-gun plodded on towards the dunes, until the stink of something both sickeningly sweet and somehow burnt stopped him short. He breasted the final dune.

He had found the missing glider. It poised there just at the water's edge, bits and pieces of equipment strewn in its wake, situated in the middle of a wide circle of blackened sand, most of its fuselage burnt away to reveal the orderly rows of charred figures, their helmets and surviving equipment loose and too large for the shrunken pygmies they had become as a result of the intense heat. Von Ernst stood there undecided, his face set in a puzzled frown. A glider had no engine, no fuel. How, then, could it have burned like that on impact with the ground?

He sniffed the air and caught a faint whiff of explosive among the sweet stench of charred human flesh. His eyes dropped to the long tube lying a few metres away. Slowly, he walked over to it and gingerly picked it up. In the light of the stars he read the name on it: '*Brandbombe*'.

'A thermite stick,' he whispered to himself, carefully placing it down again. 'Now what am I to make of this whole business? A bunch of gliderborne mountain troops carrying with them enough thermite sticks or explosives of some kind to set the whole plane alight on impact? Very strange, very strange indeed.'

Slowly, he walked a little closer to the burnt-out wreck, trying to puzzle out that overwhelming question, too deep in thought to notice the dirty white flash in the dunes to his right. He paused and struck his forehead with his clenched fist. Of course! Why hadn't he realized it before? The strange appearance of, first, the seaplane, then this transport glider, filled with dead mountaineers could mean one thing, and one thing only.

They had come to sabotage the American airfields!

[1] See *STORMTROOP* for further details.

Naturally. That was how the High Command worked. Why leave the initiative to the enemy and let them attack first? Take the war to the foe. That had always been the Prussian tradition, ever since the days of Old Fritz.

He sucked his teeth thoughtfully. But what now? The gliderborne troops had struck disaster. Suddenly, the picture of that old Auntie Ju disappearing into the cloud bank in front of the Lightnings flashed before his mind's eye. In a moment of total recall, he remembered a detail of the German transport plane he had long forgotten: *two* towing lines were hanging from the Junkers' rump. *TWO!*

'*Naturlich!*' he cried to the silver darkness and the silent corpses sitting there for eternity. 'The Junkers of the Para Corps always tow *two* gliders! There must be another one . . . *another one – which escaped*!'

He pushed himself forward towards that ghastly wreck, feeling the small hairs at the back of his neck stand erect as he came closer to those shrunken corpses fused to the metal by the heat so that they sat upright as if on parade. He swallowed hard and forced himself to reach into the charred shambles of the cockpit, a sickening sensation of revulsion almost overcoming him as he touched the dead pilot in doing so. Hastily, he swallowed the green bile which had welled up into his throat and fumbled with the blackened bits and pieces of debris on the holed floor, hoping to find something which might give him a clue to the missing glider's destination.

Nothing! The fragments of paper which had survived the fire were too charred and blackened to be of any use. He frowned and tried to shrug off the uncanny sensation that the corpses at his rear were watching him, intently following his every movement.

Then he spotted it. A pencilled outline on the crumpled aluminium of the cockpit just behind the steering column. He screwed up his eyes and tried to make it out in the silver gloom. 'M', that would be the Mediterranean. A double cross. He frowned. What could that mean? Of course, it was the way kids represent an aeroplane. It signified the Ami airfields around Benghazi. He peered more intently, following the dotted pencil-line and smudged, illegible number next to it. Now he understood what it meant. The pilot, obviously pre-occupied with the task of steering the big glider, had pencilled himself a simple flight map on the cockpit in front of him so that he didn't have to fumble with his maps once the towing plane had released him. The dotted line would be his route and the indecipherable number his bearing. Well, at least now he knew that the missing glider had intended to head due south of the Benghazi bases and from wherever it landed out there in the desert, the men aboard would march north to sabotage the US planes.

Leutnant von Ernst straightened up, the ghastly corpses to his rear forgotten. So, that was what all the activity had been about; his signals to Berlin had not been in vain. Suddenly, he felt very happy, even elated, standing there in the wreck of the plane. Fellow countrymen were out there somewhere: men who spoke his language; men who might well soon relieve him from his lonely vigil.

Von Ernst grinned up at the immense stretch of star-studded sky and was tempted to shout his triumph to it. Instead, he contented himself with a whispered, '*Es lebe Deutschland!*[1]'

It was that subdued outburst of triumph which saved his life. For in the same instant that he flung his look upwards at the sky, he glimpsed, from the corner of his eye, white-robed figures moving cautiously through the dunes. *Senussi!* Marauding Arabs who would first loot the wrecked glider and then report their discovery to the Americans for baksheesh in the form of canned corned beef and bottles of Coca Cola.

Von Ernst did not hesitate. They were almost upon him. He flung up the small American machine-pistol and pressed the trigger without aiming. It chattered into violent life at his side. The slugs stitched the silver gloom. An Arab screamed and flinging up his arms flopped to the sand

[1] 'Long live Germany.'

dramatically. Another cursed gutturally in Arabic and sat down abruptly, nursing a bloody shattered knee. But there were more coming through the dunes and they were carrying their ancient hooked rifles.

Von Ernst whipped up the hem of his robe and rubbed away the tell-tale pencilled sketch the best he could. The Amis must not find that.

A slug whined against the helmet of one of the blackened corpses and to his horror it keeled over like a dummy at a fairground shooting gallery. He left the sketch and ripped off another burst. An Arab screamed shrilly and the little group of white-robed figures which had been sneaking up on him from the other side flopped to the sands to return his fire from the prone position.

Von Ernst bit his lip. They were on both sides of him. With his wounded leg he hadn't much of a chance of nipping quickly through their positions and disappearing into the desert, he knew that. Then he thought of the sea. He'd heard that the Arabs had a loathing of water. With any luck none of them could swim. That would have to be the way out. He would swim as far out as he dare and then swim along the coast until he felt he was safe.

His decision made, von Ernst ripped off a last burst and then fitted a new magazine into the little machine-pistol. He could hear the *Senussi* creeping ever closer, the occasional slug thudding into the dead bodies all around him. He bent and started working his way between those charred horrors, using their dead flesh as a primitive form of protection. The Arabs were closing in. Von Ernst smiled. He knew their tactics. They would attempt to get as close as possible before rising to their feet and making a rush for him; that way they'd avoid too many casualties. And expecting others to act as cautiously as themselves, they wouldn't expect anyone to do what he was now going to do.

He took a deep breath and then with the grease-gun clamped firmly to his hip, he darted from the wrecked glider, firing as he ran. An Arab sprang up from the sand, screaming furiously. Something silver gleamed in his upraised hand. Von Ernst swung the grease-gun round. The Arab reeled back, his face ripped apart by the slugs at close range, bright scarlet blood jetting from a dozen holes. Another rose to his knees and raised his ancient rifle. Von Ernst didn't give him a chance to fire it. He swung the grease-gun like a bat. The rifle flew from the surprised Arab's fingers. Next instant, von Ernst had rammed the metal butt into his face. He screamed shrilly, his nose smashed, blood spurting from his shattered mouth.

A handful of Arabs sprang from the dunes to his right. Flinging away their rifles they started to run clumsily through the heavy sand. Von Ernst reacted first. Carried away by a crazed blood-lust, he pressed his trigger. The grease-gun chattered frantically. They went down in a confused heap of flailing arms and legs, screaming with pain, writhing in the sand in their death agonies. Von Ernst pelted on.

Now the sand was firmer under his flying feet. Before him the sea gleamed in the silver light. He had nearly done it! An Arab broke from the cover of the dunes to his right. Von Ernst pressed his trigger. Nothing happened! He pressed it again, cursing himself. The magazine was empty.

The Arab ran for him, his dark face contorted and triumphant, as he realized that the man running for the sea was defenceless now. He halted and raised his rifle, taking his time, savouring his victory, knowing that von Ernst was completely at his mercy.

Von Ernst reacted instinctively. He flung the useless machine-pistol. He was lucky. The weapon struck the Arab right in the face. He reeled back, his rifle falling to the sand. Von Ernst didn't give him a chance to recover and pick it up. He flung himself forward in a tremendous shallow dive. The water struck him a murderous blow in the pit of the stomach. But he had no time to think of the pain. With all his remaining strength he started swimming furiously, keeping as low as possible, praying that they wouldn't follow, hearing them rush into the water and the *phut-phut* of their slugs hitting the waves all around him. And then he had done it and was out of range, their cries of frustrated rage music to his ears, as he kept on swimming further and further into the sweet protection of the darkening sea . . .

FOUR

Now it was midday. The sun hung like a molten lead ball in a dark, threatening sky. The wind blew. But it brought no relief from the heat, for it was hot and sticky. A storm was brewing.

Undaunted, the hungry, weary mountaineers made their preparations for the one hot meal of the day. Sand was scooped up and dropped into the bottom of large food cans. Then their precious petrol was carefully poured in and stirred with the sand, until a consistency of thick oatmeal porridge had been achieved.

Matches were then struck downwind and gingerly tossed into the mixture. A soft whoosh of blue flame and the cans began to burn. The stoves were ready to cook the midday meal, which, as usual, was 'Old Man'.[1]

Stuermer watched his men's preparations for a while, then once again he felt that uneasy sensation in his lower bowel which he had been experiencing ever since they had set off on their long march north, twenty-four hours ago. His 'gippo squitters', as his mountaineers were already calling the infection, was back once again. Hurriedly he collected some lavatory paper and an entrenching tool and said to Greul, 'Your turn to cook the Old Man, Greul. I have an appointment over there.' He pulled a wry face. 'Got to take the shovel for a walk once more.'

Greul nodded his understanding. Half the men were already suffering from the same complaint, carried from man to man by the damned irritating flies which swarmed everywhere. Stuermer did not wait to see if Greul needed any further instructions. Instead he sped away and once he

[1] Standard Germany Army meat ration, reputedly made from old men collected in Berlin's old folks' homes.

was over the nearest dune and out of sight of his grinning troopers, he broke into a run towards the shelter of a large boulder. With a sigh of relief, he ripped open his khaki trousers, spade held like a weapon in his hands, and got down to the pressing business of nature.

Around him the wind whipped up the sand in wild little flurries and he narrowed his eyes to slits every now and again as sand was blown into his face. He frowned and started to wield his shovel. They were in for a sand storm and he knew from his experiences in the Gobi Desert before the war, that, at this time of the year, a sandstorm could be a killing business if a man didn't take the right precautions.

As quickly as he could, bent double now against the force of the wind, which buffeted him in the face with blows like a clenched fist, he staggered back the way he had come, knowing that he had to get back immediately to warn the men – and also before his own tracks, which he was now following, were not obliterated.

He stumbled over the last dune and glimpsed his men through the flying whirling cloud of vicious yellow sand. They stared at him aghast, as if he were the cause of this tremendous frightening storm.

Stuermer cupped his hands around his mouth, feeling the hot wind sucking the very air from his lungs. 'Get down, everybody!' he cried. '*DOWN!*'

He staggered down into the camp. 'Cling to the men next to you!' he yelled above the murderous howl of the wind. 'Don't let yourselves be separated on any account. Get together now!'

He dropped at Greul's side and grasped his arm. 'Hold on!' he commanded desperately as the storm engulfed them at full force, '*HERE WE GO!*'

At one hundred and fifty kilometres an hour, the *khamsin* struck them like a wall of hot knives, lashing at their horrified faces with lethal ferocity. Sand particles peppered their bodies through the thin desert uniform. They howled with pain. But the wind snatched the words from their mouths and filled their lungs with sand.

Breathing became virtually impossible. The hellish, howling yellow fog snatched the very air from their lungs. They gasped and choked like asthmatics in the paroxysms of an attack.

On and on the dreadful storm continued. Its ululating threnody rose to an ever louder pitch. It was deafening, frightening, murderous. The *khamsin* had travelled across two thousand kilometres of uncharted desert to strike this miserable handful of two-legged creatures cowering for their lives and it was not going to be denied its victims.

Desperately, the men clung together like lost children, sobbing with fear, uttering meaningless terrified sounds as the great wind struck them time and time again.

Once, Stuermer attempted to open his eyes and penetrate the flying wall of sand. But he was compelled to close them again immediately, his eyes full of coarse burning particles. Fearfully he ducked his head even more and clung on to a howling Grcul for dear life.

With renewed force the *khamsin* struck them once again. Stuermer heard a muffled scream and had the impression of something brushing by him. Perhaps one of his men was being carried away by that merciless wind. But he could not open his burning eyes to look. He said a quick prayer that he might be wrong.

With renewed force the great wind struck them yet once more, shrieking and wailing furiously across the face of the desert, as if some god on high had decreed that these puny mortals should be wiped from the face of the earth because of their temerity in penetrating his burning kingdom. It seemed never-ending. Crouched low, by now half buried in the sand, Stuermer wanted to shake himself free of it and scream that it must stop. *STOP!*

And then, as abruptly as it had commenced, the terrifying, maddening howl gave way to a soft mournful dirge that decreased by the instant, until finally it stopped altogether, leaving behind it a chilling, soft echo. Silence hung over the desert once more.

It seemed to take a long long time for the sand-covered soldiers to recover from the shock of the great storm and realize that it was over, as if they did not dare believe that their ordeal was passed. Finally like blind men, they started to pat and feel their sand-caked bodies, clawing at their faces to remove the clinging particles, taking deep grateful gulps of the cooler air.

Stuermer forced himself up to a sitting position, hearing the sand shower from his upper body. He felt for his burning eyes and rubbed them clear, snorting through his sand-choked nostrils as he did so.

Opposite him Ox-Jo sat up, his broad face solidly encrusted in glittering new sand. The big NCO ran his pink tongue along his parched lips. A thick wet streak of red broke the yellow mask that covered his face. He coughed thickly and said, 'Christ on a crutch, I thought they'd croaked me for sure that time.' He coughed yet once again and spat into the dust.

Wearily Stuermer rose to his feet. He stared around his little command. 'Clean up,' he commanded throatily, 'and report . . . Do you hear, clean up—' He stopped short with a gasp of fear, all storm-induced lethargy vanished in an instant.

In a full circle right around the little camp, there were camels crouched in the gleaming new sand and lying behind each camel, long ancient curved rifles levelled menacingly at the men of Stormtroop Edelweiss, were skinny dark men, the lower half of their faces covered by blue veils, their eyes hard and unwinking.

Slowly, very slowly, all hope draining from his big body, Colonel Stuermer started to raise his hands in surrender. All around him his men began to do the same.

They staggered ever forward like drunken men, occasionally sprawling full length in the burning sand. But not for long. The cruel rope that dug deep into their bound wrists dragged them on, until somehow or other they managed to stumble once more to their feet.

Above them the bright yellow ball of the sun thrashed them mercilessly with its burning light so that their bodies ran constantly with sweat under their tattered, clinging uniforms.

'They're Tuaregs, I think,' Stuermer gasped to Greul as they half-trotted, half-slithered behind the camel to which they were tied. 'Judging by their veils that is.'

'Are they friendly to the Amis?' Greul croaked hoarsely, the blood still trickling down from the wound they had inflicted with their goads on his forehead.

'I don't know,' Stuermer gasped, preventing himself from falling just in time. 'All I know about them is that they are the dominant nomads of the central and western Sahara.' He winced with pain as the camel stumbled and the rope tautened, digging deep into his already bloody wrists. 'I think they also wander along the Middle Niger from Timbuktu to Nigeria, doing a little slave trading—'

'Slave trading!' Greul gasped, looking at Stuermer with his blood-shot eyes full of horror. 'But we are Germans, not a bunch of niggers!'

Stuermer ignored the comment; he was too weary to protest. 'My guess is that they do pretty much as they damn well like, owing allegiance to no man but themselves, fighting to survive the best they can in this waste.'

'But why take us prisoner?'

'Why?' Stuermer echoed. 'Because we are a commodity, just as they regard their cattle, camels and other livestock as commodities. They'll sell us in the best market place available, alive – *or dead*!'

Towards late afternoon the camels started to quicken their pace without any goading from their veiled riders, dragging the half-conscious, blood-spattered Germans behind.

'Water,' Stuermer said thickly, being forced into a shambling, rubber-legged run. 'They must have scented water somewhere.' He eyed the burning blue haze to their front and thought he saw a faint smudge to the left which might indicate an oasis.

'Thank God!' Greul gasped, running like a splay-footed, newly-born foal at his side. 'I don't think I can keep this up much longer.'

An hour later the utterly exhausted, dehydrated men, their tongues hanging out of their gaping mouths like dried leather straps, saw before their blurred eyes a huge stretch of enormous, granite boulders. And in the centre lay a patch of bright green. Stuermer blinked his eyes a couple of times, hardly daring to believe what they saw – a clump of swaying elegant date palms!

He swallowed with difficulty, and thought with almost a sexual longing of the shade they would afford and the water which must supply them. *Water!* Clear cool water, litre upon litre of it, sluicing his parched throat. Drinking until his belly was grossly distended like that of a woman far gone in pregnancy.

Ten minutes later, with the last of their fast-vanishing strength, they started to agonize their way through the rocky garden of madness, twisting and turning with the greedy camels through the huge boulders, gazes fixed on the green palms hungrily, as if they marked the gate to Paradise itself.

And then they were through, staggering and stumbling into a camp of black cloth tents arranged beneath the trees. Beady-eyed, unwinking children, half-naked and with bellies distended from lack of proper nourishment, watched their entrance; and women, unveiled as was the custom of the Tuaregs, squatted on their haunches, fanning cooking fires with palm fronds.

At last it was over. The camels were released and fled in an awkward scamper for the water. The exhausted soldiers fell where they stood, their wrists still cruelly tied together, heads sunk in defeat.

For a little while their captors watched them with their cruel black eyes, the eyes of men who had sold slaves for centuries, and then without leaving a single sentry to guard the troopers stalked into the tented encampment with the proud arrogant strides of men who had something to boast about.

Night came with the startling suddenness of the desert. The hapless prisoners who had been given a gourd of tepid water each an hour before by the half-naked children, who had danced tauntingly in front of them as they had done so, started to shiver.

Stuermer, huddled next to Greul, stared at the flickering fires of the camp fifty metres away or so and thought with longing of the warmth those camel-dung fires provided, as his nostrils were assailed by the smell of camel-meat cooking. He forced himself to forget food and warmth and concentrate on the problem at hand.

Their captors now had sentries out, not many, but they were armed with the machine-pistols they had taken from their prisoners. The Schmeissers had caused a great hullabaloo when one of them had accidentally pressed his trigger and sent an electric stream of white tracer hissing into the sky. Even though the guards were veiled, it was easy to see their pride in these powerful new weapons and Stuermer had no doubt they would handle them competently if necessary.

Carefully, Greul pressed his lips close to Stuermer's right ear, not for one moment taking his eyes off the nearest guard while all around them the exhausted troopers tossed and turned and moaned in a fitful sleep. 'What do you make of it, Colonel?' he whispered carefully.

Stuermer, who had never felt so hopeless in all his life, forced himself to answer with military precision. 'One, I think I know where we are. Those boulders were the clue. It's called the Devil's Garden and it's just at the edge of the unexplored part of the Sahara. Two, it's some three hundred kilometres south of Benghazi. Three, my guess is the Tuaregs won't take us north with them, but south into Central Africa—'

Greul gasped. 'You mean to sell us as slaves?'

Stuermer nodded sombrely. 'I think so. The Americans might pay them a reward for having captured us, but they won't realize the price for us we'd bring on the slave market – and remember most European nations have been fighting the slave trade for over a century. They'll be suspicious of all whites.'

Greul absorbed the information, while closer to the oasis one of the tribesmen's skinny-ribbed, frightened dogs howled at the sky. 'They didn't find the gold,' he whispered after a moment. 'It's hidden in my money belt. Perhaps—'

'They'll take the gold and *still* sell us as slaves,' Stuermer cut him short. 'They are that kind of people, Greul. Their code of conduct is completely different to ours. No, that's not the way. If we're gonna get out of this mess, we're going to have to do it by sheer force of arms. It's the only language those veiled devils understand. We've got to get free by our own efforts.'

Greul nodded gloomily, 'I see what you mean, sir. The question is – *how*?'

It was the same overwhelming question which preoccupied Ox-Jo and Jap tied together to a desert palm some fifty metres away. Just after they had been released from the bondage of the camels, Ox-Jo had lashed out with the last of his strength and sent one of the Tuaregs flying in the sand. The man had recovered quickly, drawn his curved knife and would have plunged it into the big man's heart on the spot, if it had not been for his fellow tribesmen. They had restrained him with difficulty. But as punishment for his offence, he and Jap had been tied back to back to the tree and disallowed their ration of water.

Now while their comrades moaned and groaned in a restless sleep all around them in the glowing velvet gloom of a desert night, the two of them racked their brains for a way to free themselves in order to slake their raging thirst; for neither of them had had a drink since before the sandstorm.

In the end it was little half-breed Jap who had the idea

which would save what was left of Stormtroop Edelweiss. 'Listen, Ox,' he whispered furtively, keeping his eye on the nearest guard who was crouched over his fire, smoking one of his captives' cigarettes, 'I've just remembered.'

'What yer remembered, you asparagus Tarzan – that you've got a pressing appointment in a Munich whorehouse?' Ox-Jo snorted.

'Knock it off, plush-ears – and listen.' Jap lowered his voice even more. 'You remember those L-pills[1] they gave us in Berlin?'

'Go on, we flung 'em away once we boarded the gliders, just as the CO ordered us to do. He said none of us would ever use them as long as he commanded Stormtroop Edelweiss and—'

'I know, I know,' Jap hissed urgently. 'Will ya hold yer water and listen! But I didn't like the idea of not having some way of getting – well you know what I mean, you big horned ox. So I provided my own L-pill.'

'By the Great God and All His Triangles, what in hell's name are you rabbiting on about?'

'Under the instep of my boot, taped on by some sticking plaster, I've got a razor blade.'

'*What*—'

'Holy cow, shut it up, will you!' Jap said hurriedly. 'Yer don't want to wake up the whole shitting camp, do you? I'll say it agen, nice and slowly. There's a safety-razor blade taped to my right dice-beaker. Now—'

'Speak no more. If we can get to your boot, we're on our way.'

'Yes, in one. The only problem is how to get to my dice-beaker, trussed up like we are?'

Ox-Jo's big, bluff Bavarian face sank. 'Yer, that's where we're really caught by the short and curlies.'

For a long while the two of them slumped there back to back against the rough-ribbed date palm trunk, sunk in

[1] Suicide or 'lethal' pills given to German soldiers on special missions so that they might do away with themselves if caught.

gloom, the only sound the howl of the dogs and the steady crackle of the camel-dung fire.

Then suddenly Jap had it. 'Imagine going into a chimney climb, arse first, Ox, what do you do?' he broke the heavy silence with the strange query.

'You rupture yourself trying to turn arse-over-tip, supporting yersen with yer pinkies, yer back against the rock face, upside down with yer legs spread in the air like a pavement-pounder on her back waiting for a nice big thick piece of human salami. Why?'

'*Why?*' Jap echoed excitedly. 'Because this tree trunk could act as a rock face. Now if I could manage to get myself base over apex, you could use yer choppers and pluck the blade from my instep.'

'Holy strawsack, Jap, you little half-cast shit, I think you've got it,' Ox-Jo agreed in an excited whisper. 'Do you think you can make it?'

'I've gotta, Ox,' Jap answered, his voice betraying real fear for the first time. 'Cos if I don't, I wouldn't give yer a monkey's for our future. Come on. You're facing the nigger. Keep yer glassy orbits on him, while I go into my circus act. Now!'

While Ox-Jo watched the nearest sentry with almost hypnotic force, Jap took his time, then with a sudden gasp, flung up his legs. His boots struck the tree trunk softly. '*Now*,' he urged once more through gritted teeth, trying to maintain his feet in position as long as possible.

Ox-Jo strained his head to one side, teeth bared, craning his neck millimetre by millimetre, edging ever closer to the white blur of the blade taped to Jap's instep. He almost had it, when Jap gave a groan and let his feet fall heavily. 'Sorry, Ox,' he gasped, sucking in a deep breath of air hurriedly, 'just couldn't hold on any longer. I was choking.'

'It's all right, Jap, give yersen a minute and we'll try again.' Three times they tried and then finally Ox-Jo felt the sharp pain of a keen blade cutting into his lips and the sudden flush of warm blood in his mouth. He stifled the yelp of pain just in time and hissed through his bleeding lips, 'Let go . . . let go, Jap!'

Jap let his legs drop gratefully and again Ox-Jo fought back the cry of pain, as the blade was ripped off and fell onto his tongue. Next instant he was bending his head, and spitting out the blood-stained blade within grasping distance of Jap's bound right hand. 'It's all yours, Jap,' he whispered, swallowing the hot blood. 'Get the lead out of yer arse and get cutting!'

Jap needed no urging. His small, cunning fingers sought and found the blade. He wiped the slippery blood from it, the best he could, then frowning hard, knowing that he was going to cut his own fingers terribly while carrying out his vital task, he started to saw and saw Ox-Jo's bonds. The rescue attempt had commenced . . .

FIVE

It was nearly dawn. The tented camp had sunk into a heavy sleep. Even the dogs were silent. The only sounds were the snores of the sleeping tribesmen and their womenfolk, and the soft rustle of the date palms in the night breeze.

But all were not sleeping in the oasis. Furtive figures moved through the gloom, taking the positions ordained by the soft whisper from man to man. Everywhere there was silent fearful movement.

Stuermer narrowed his eyes to slits, trying to penetrate the dirty white pre-dawn gloom; for now the stars had long disappeared. As far as he could make out his men, happy at being released, their ordeal forgotten now, seemed to be in position. He swallowed hard and hesitated momentarily. They were completely unarmed. It was bare hands against the looted automatics of the tribesmen. It needed only one small slip-up and a massacre would take place in this remote oasis. They would not be given a second chance. He licked suddenly parched lips and made his decision. 'All right, Ox, off you go,' he commanded in a hoarse whisper. 'And watch out for yourself.'

'I will, sir, never fear.' Ox nudged his running-mate. 'All right, arse with ears. You heard the CO. Let's make dust.'

Silently, amazingly silently for such a big man, Ox started crawling forward towards the nearest sentry sunk in a deep sleep, followed by Jap.

Stuermer watched them go for an instant before they disappeared into the gloom and then raising his head gave the call of the alpine buzzard, the agreed-upon signal for action.

Now dark figures everywhere started to crawl the last

few metres to their allotted targets, while Stuermer held his breath, tense with anxiety, knowing that the next few minutes might well decide the fate of forty good men.

In the thin, white light, Ox-Jo could make out every detail of the veiled face, the dark beetle-brows above the half-concealed hawk of a nose, the high cheekbones, the sallow, pock-marked skin. There was no mistaking it. The face of the sleeping sentry was that of a warrior, descended from generations of warriors, and on his robed lap rested the Schmeisser machine-pistol ready for action. One slip-up, he told himself, and Frau Meier's handsome son is for the chop.

Slowly, his heart thumping anxiously like a pump with tension, he started to crawl the last few metres which separated him from the sleeping sentry, keeping well below his line of vision in case he suddenly woke up. When almost within grasping distance, he raised his right hand which held a large rock. It was his only weapon. '*One . . . two . . . th—*'

He began to count off the seconds, hand raised ready for the brutal dirty business ahead.

The sentry stirred. Dully, he began to open his eyes, his trigger finger instinctively curling around his machine-pistol. His dark eyes flickered open. He saw Ox-Jo crouching there, rock in hand. He opened his mouth to cry alarm. Too late! Ox-Jo hit him a tremendous blow with the rock. His skull gave an audible crack. Black blood spurted from his nostrils and splattered the front of Ox-Jo's shirt as he brought the rock down once more, and the sentry keeled over flat on his face, unconscious or dead.

Greedily, Ox-Jo grabbed for his Schmeisser and waved it in signal to Jap who was crouched behind him as back-up. And the two of them started to stalk the second sentry, who was sleeping, squatted on his haunches, closer to the camp.

This time, however, their luck ran out. Just when they were within striking range, there came a thin wail from the nearest black tent. There was no mistaking that cry. It was the shrill, high-pitched scream of a woman in the moment of supreme ecstasy. 'Lucky bugger!' Ox-Jo cried foolishly at the top of his voice. The sentry started out of his sleep and Ox-Jo simultaneously pressed the trigger of the Schmeisser.

At such short range, he couldn't miss. The burst of slugs lifted the man right off the ground and then slammed him down once more, leaking blood from a line of red buttonholes suddenly stitched the length of his chest.

'Grab his popgun, Jap!' Ox-Jo bellowed, knowing now that there was no further need for silence as excited cries, curses, commands in the guttural African tongue rose on all sides.

Together, he and Jap raced for the tents, pumping quick controlled bursts to left and right, kicking at the tent ropes as they ran, turning the camp into chaos. Dark-skinned men, women and children were fleeing everywhere only to be met by the waiting troopers who fell on the men who had tortured them so cruelly on the long trek through the desert, hurling them to the ground and ripping the weapons out of their hands. The dawn air was filled with guttural yells, cries of agonized pain and deep atavistic grunts of satisfaction as yet another torturer was felled for good.

In the end, as the red ball of the sun loomed up on the horizon uncertainly, as if it were hesitating to light up this grim scene of murder and mayhem below, Stuermer had to step in and order his men to stop before they were carried away by their blood-rage and commenced murdering the terrified women and children.

By six that morning, at the cost of one man dead and six lightly wounded, the oasis known as the 'Devil's Garden' was firmly in the hands of the stormtroopers, with the surviving males tied in the same way they had tied up the Edelweiss men, dark eyes flashing fire over their veils, roles completely reversed now.

For a while the excited, sweat-streaked victors concerned themselves with the pure joy of guzzling the sparkling, icy-cold well water, while the dark-clad women wailed and threw dust in their faces in the Arab fashion, and their puzzled children sobbed softly at their sides.

Then sitting down, stomachs distended, they turned to listen to their orders from Major Greul, who somewhere or other had found an ancient cut-throat razor and shaved away five days's growth of beard, thus leaving a curve of pale white skin which contrasted strangely with his dark-brown tan.

'We shall move out as soon as we have collected our supplies and as much water as we can carry. I have discussed the matter with the CO. We shall take their camels from them and use them as transport. Now there will be no need to hide during the day. With the camels and their robes, we will be taken by any observer from the air or from any distance as just another bunch of nomadic tribesmen.'

Ox-Jo, happily munching a huge bunch of sticky sweet dates, the juice running down his dark unshaven chin, nudged Jap and whispered. 'There you are. Now we've got the mustard! We're going to end up as donkey wallopers, as I always predicted we would. What an Army – a lot of maidservants to a shitting lot of mangy-looking creatures with the hump!'

But that was not to be, for in that same instant, some five hundred metres away, hidden from the rest by one of the huge boulders, Colonel Stuermer was staring as if mesmerized at the huge truck parked at the bottom of a sharp incline which led out of the oasis.

It was of a kind that he had never seen before. Built so that its axles were well clear of the sand, it had both wheels and small tracks so that it appeared to be a kind of primitive half-track. But what was it doing here, he asked himself, as he slipped the safety catch off his machine-pistol and advanced upon the strange-looking truck warily, weapon at the ready.

As he got closer, he could see that it had been there a long time, a very long time. Its sides were weathered a dull white by the desert wind and the hard metallic paint, which had once covered its sloping engine bonnet, had almost vanished, leaving behind the naked steel below exposed. The fading letters, CITROËN, however, were still just decipherable.

Cautiously, he tugged at the door which was level with his head and stumbled backwards, nearly falling as he did so, when the door came off in his hand.

Colonel Stuermer frowned and stared inside the cab, the leather of the seats was torn and cracked, with the springs and horse-hair showing everywhere. And sand had drifted in until it was ankle-deep. Suddenly, he spotted the scrap of yellowed, brittle paper. He picked it up and just as it disintegrated in his hand, he caught the name and the date. *Le Monde, Juin 1928.*

He whistled softly through his teeth. *The big antiquated Citroën had been here in the desert for over fifteen years!*

'It's the bone-dry air and the sand,' Colonel Stuermer explained to the gaping troopers as they gathered around the big truck, regarding it with awe, as they might have some primeval mammoth. 'It preserves things like this for centuries. I recall once talking to an officer of the Afrika Korps, who while out on patrol in early '42 came across a British armoured car which had been abandoned in the desert in their campaign against the Turks in 1916 – and it started perfectly after all those years!' he hesitated and staring at the awed faces of his men, saw that the last days in the desert had taken their toll. Most of them were blackened death's heads, with their eyes blood-shot by the sun's glare, and bulging through exhaustion and lack of proper food. 'I make no promises, but if we could start that monster there – I've checked, its tanks are almost three-quarters full with fuel – it would—'

'Save a shitting lot of footslogging through this shitting sand!' Ox-Jo beat him to it with an enthusiastic bellow.

Stuermer grinned. 'Right as always, Meier. As you phrase it so delicately, it *shittingly* well would!'

The men grinned and Jap asked. 'But how did it get here, sir?' Such things always troubled the half-breed; he was prey to all kinds of superstitions.

Stuermer shrugged. 'Couldn't say exactly. Back in the late twenties the French government ran what they called Trans-Sahara expeditions into the desert from North Africa to open up the desert, make an overland route to their colonies in Central Africa possible, and to impress the desert Arabs who were giving them and the Spaniards a lot of trouble about that time. But how this particular Citroën got here is beyond me.'

'And the crew?' Jap persisted.

Greul held up his hand which he had kept concealed behind his back while Stuermer had been talking. In it a gleaming white skull, the bones polished by nearly two decades of shifting sand, grinned down at the little half-breed.

Jap shivered violently and Major Greul said harshly. 'This might be the answer. Those murderous niggers were undoubtedly responsible for whatever treacherous business took place here back in 1928. The whole rotten pack of them should—'

Stuermer held up his hand for silence. 'Now, men we have the choice. There are the camels or this wheeled monster, providing we can get it running again. What is it going to be? Hooves or wheels?

'*WHEELS!*' came back the enthusiastic, unanimous roar which set the curs back in the tented village barking and whining fearfully.

'*Wheels any time, sir!*'

Stuermer grinned. 'All right, comrades, prepare to get your hands dirty – and your backs broken. We've got a lot of work to do, for you see, I haven't told you the worse bit yet.'

Ox-Jo clapped his hand to his forehead and gave a mock groan. 'I knew, I crappingly well knew it! Yer never get anything for nothing in this man's army. What is it?'

'You see that slope up there. Well, we've got to – once

we manage to clean and prepare the engine – somehow or other, get this monster up there. I've tried the engine and it won't start. I'm hoping that it will on the downward slope. But first we have to get the beast, and my guess is that it weighs ten ton, up that damned hill!'

Ox-Jo followed the direction of Colonel Stuermer's outstretched hand and moaned, 'Look at it, will ya. It's like Everest! I swear, I'll shit a brick, I swear I will . . .!'

Sergeant-Major Ox-Jo Meier didn't know the half of it.

SIX

Ox-Jo wiped his hands on his robe – they were all now wearing robes as a precaution against enemy reconnaissance planes flying over the oasis – and made his announcement. 'I'm getting a spark from two of the plugs, although the battery's flatter than the tits on a Hitler Maiden.'

Greul frowned and Stuermer smiled at the comparison, but neither said anything as they stood there in the boiling heat listening.

'The oil in the sump was a bit low, but I drained the oil from one of the motorbikes and added that. Now it's all right. The water in the radiator has long evaporated, but I filled it up again and it's not leaking.' He paused momentarily and flung an apprehensive glance at the slope to the rear, now rippling with little blue waves from the murderous midday heat. 'In short, sir, the bitch is ready to go – once we get her up there.'

Stuermer's grin vanished. 'All right, bring up the prisoners!' he commanded.

Under guard, a dozen Arabs, their dark eyes bitter and resentful, staggered to the waiting Germans, each one carrying two heavy rocks.

'Now,' Stuermer lectured the two teams into which he had divided Stormtroop Edelweiss, 'each group shoves for five minutes. Immediately they are ready to cease, the Arabs are to be ordered to place their rocks beneath the rear tracks to stop the vehicle rolling backwards. And you, Jap' – being the smallest member of Stormtroop Jap would do the steering – 'remember to hit the brakes at once.'

'Will do, sir,' Jap agreed happily, knowing that he had won himself a reprieve from the back-breaking task ahead.

He winked at Ox-Jo and whispered, 'Get to the oars, galley-slave.'

The big NCO poked up a middle finger that looked like a small pork sausage. 'Sit on that, you poison-dwarf!' he growled.

'Can't. Already got a Berlin double-decker bus up there.'

Stuermer nodded to his team, which was to be the first. 'All right, comrades, here we go. Jap, jump in!'

The little half-breed needed no urging. He swung himself up and into the cab with the agility of a mountain goat and yelped when in the next instant he touched the burning hot wheel. He grabbed the massive handbrake. For a moment it refused to budge. Finally a hefty kick with his mountain boot shifted it. '*Fertig!*' he sang out happily and prepared to steer the monster up the steep slope ahead.

'*Los!*' Stuermer warned his team and, turning, wedged his broad back against the right end of the truck '*JETZT!*'

Twenty hardy, muscular mountaineers heaved. Nothing happened. The truck stubbornly refused to budge.

Stuermer tried again. '*Hau-ruck!*' he commanded through gritted teeth, the veins standing out at his temples, his face a deep brick-red.

There was a stiff creak. Springs that had not moved for nearly two decades squeaked in rusty protest. There was a sucking sound as the wheels fought the clinging grip of the deep sand.

'She's moving, the bitch!' Ox-Jo cried in triumph, '*she's moving*!' He gave another tremendous push and the rotten wood of the panel cracked like a rifle shot. Ox-Jo cursed and caught himself from falling just in time.

For five long minutes, the Stuermer team pushed and shoved and heaved, moving the 10-ton monster up the slope, millimetre by millimetre, until finally in a choking dying voice, Stuermer cried, 'Stones . . . For Crissake, get the stones up here!'

One instant later, he and the rest had collapsed flat on their faces in the sand, shoulders heaving madly as if they had just run a great race, while the Arabs wedged stones frantically under the Citroën's wheels to prevent it rolling backwards . . .

All that afternoon they laboured up that slope like slaves in the times of the Pharaohs, building the Great Pyramids. As they toiled ever upwards under that murderous burning sun, their breath came in great hectic gasps, the veins at their temples hammering away madly as if they might well burst out at any moment.

Now it had taken on the qualities of a nightmare, pierced by the physical pain of their effort: the raw bruises on the shoulders, the torn ripped nails, the sunburnt, raw backs, the sand particles matted to sweat-soaked faces – and always that maddening command, '*Los jetzt . . . hau-ruck!*', which ordered them to stumble blindly to their feet and face the torture yet again.

By four o'clock they were still fifty metres from the summit. And the going had got tougher: the sand had become deep and soft so that the wheels sank into it, hindering progress.

Stuermer, at the end of his tether, and knowing that his men wouldn't last much longer, was forced to be absolutely ruthless. 'Get the women out of the tents,' he snarled, wiping the dripping sweat from his crimson face. 'And their damned kids, too. Hurry!'

Swiftly, the mountaineers rounded up anyone capable of working and, prodding the weeping, protesting civilians up the slope, explained what they had to do in a dumb pantomime.

The last lap of that impossible ascent had commenced. With Jap at the wheel, bellowing directions, the women dug a trough in the deep sand, and filled it with reed mats and skins taken from their tents. Then holding the skins taut they waited till the tyres took a grip. To the rear the two teams laboured, flinging themselves flat on their faces in the churned up sand, their limbs trembling like aspen leaves under the almost impossible strain, staggering through their labour blindly like old men with the burning eyes of the insane.

By ten o'clock they had done it. After an eternity of pushing, panting and cursing they finally got the monster to the top of the incline. And then, Arab and German alike, collapsed, the air wheezing through their strained lungs.

Stuermer gave them fifteen minutes, while he leaned against the truck wheezing like an asthmatic in the throes of an attack, staring unseeingly at the shimmering desert plain beyond.

Finally, he had controlled his breathing and the trembling in his limbs sufficiently to be able to croak, 'All right, on yer feet – and get those Arabs up as well!'

There were groans and protests, but Jap, the only one of them still fresh enough to do so, went among them striking their prostrate bodies with his boot, forcing them to their feet, till they stood there swaying unsteadily from side to side.

'All right, once more – and get the Arabs at it too.' He stared around at their sweat-lathered faces. 'Didn't you hear me, you bunch of piss pansies!' he snarled. 'Get behind the bitch again and when I tell you – *heave*!'

Wearily the men took up their positions once more.

'Jap, are you ready?'

'Sir.' The little half-breed pushed the clutch home and switched on the dead ignition. Taking the wooden mallet he had found in the Citroën's tool kit he hammered the lever into second gear. 'Ready when you are, sir!' he shouted, poising intently over the wheel.

'*HEAVE!*' Stuermer croaked.

They heaved. The truck cleared the summit. For one moment a helpless Stuermer thought it wasn't going to move any further, for it seemed to hesitate. But no, slowly, but surely it started downwards. 'Here we go!' Jap cried excitedly, as it began to lumber on, carried downwards by sheer weight alone. Faster and faster.

'Watch that shitting boulder!' Ox-Jo cried anxiously.

But Jap had already seen it. He swung the wheel to the

right, at the very last moment, and missed the two-metre-high boulder by a hair's breadth.

The truck was doing about twenty kilometres an hour. Stuermer, digging the nails of one hand into the raw palm of the other, willed her desperately to start.

Jap said a quick prayer and then lifted his foot off the clutch. The truck heaved violently. A thick black oily cloud erupted in a tight mushroom from the exhaust. Nothing happened! The motor had failed to start!

Stuermer moaned, and Ox-Jo smashed a big angry fist against the trunk of the palm tree under which he was sheltered.

With about fifty metres of the descent left now before the flat desert beyond, the truck began to gather speed again. Stuermer bit his bottom lip till the blood came. It was now or never!

There was a low eerie groan. It went on and on. Black smoke started to stream from the exhaust. The whine grew into an intense, ear-splitting keening. He swallowed hard. There were only twenty metres of slope left now. He tensed every nerve. The noise grew ever shriller. The truck started to shake and rattle at every seam. It seemed as if it might explode and disintegrate at any moment. Ten metres . . . only ten metres left. A series of backfires. White smoke spurted from the exhaust in a mad rush. Violent, electric-blue sparks followed. The rattling grew ever wilder. And suddenly there was the tremendous roar of a powerful engine. In an instant the truck was moving forward under its own power, with the men cheering wildly, jumping up and down.

Stuermer sat down, suddenly, with a moan. Next to him Ox-Jo said weakly, 'I'm sure I've pissed myself!' But the men, their exhaustion forgotten now, were stumbling, rolling, falling down the steep slope to where Jap, his yellow face wreathed in a huge smile of triumph, was stationary, gunning the engine for all he was worth.

They had done it. *They had wheels!*

SEVEN

Jap, Stuermer, Greul and Ox-Jo crowded into the big cab of the Citroën, with Ox-Jo singing away happily about the 'maiden', who 'could never be satisfied' till one day she was 'confronted with the prick of steel', much to the disgust of the prudish Major next to him.

Ever since they had started just after dark, leaving the Arabs weaponless, the twenty-year-old vehicle had stood up well to the horrific terrain; though they had had a few anxious moments on the occasional slope when it had shuddered frighteningly like some very weary and ancient animal about to give up the ghost and die.

More than once, of course, they had been bogged down by the sand, which meant that every man was forced to dig furiously with their entrenching tools to free the sunken rear axle. A couple of times, too, they had edged along dunes twenty metres high, bumping and banging their way along the tops of the craters, their foreheads streaming with sweat, every second expecting to roll over the side and end up with broken necks at the bottom.

'*I'm satisfied, the maiden screamed. But the prick of steel* . . .' Ox-Jo chortled merrily, while Stuermer took his eyes off the glowing, green compass needle momentarily and turning to Greul said, 'We'll drive till dawn, then lay up after cooking a meal, for the day. Somehow or other we'll camouflage the truck.'

'You think we're getting near to them now, do you, sir?' Greul asked, frowning at the singing NCO, without success. 'The Amis, I mean.'

'Yes, at this rate and without any prolonged stops, I reckon we'll cover about a hundred and fifty kilometres by first light. Thirty-six hours from dawn tomorrow we should

– God willing – be within striking distance of the main Benghazi field.'

'Excellent, excellent,' Greul snapped promptly, forgetting Ox-Jo's obscene song even, in a burst of sudden enthusiasm. 'Things are turning out better than we thought, sir, eh?'

Stuermer frowned and replaced his gaze on the glowing compass needle. 'So far, so good, Greul. But remember there is many a slip between the cup and the lip. We have a long way to go yet – a very long way.'

'*In and out, it went*,' Ox-Jo sang lustily, '*the prick of steel . . .*'

They drove on steadily through the night, Greul and Ox-Jo slumped on each other's shoulders, their old animosity forgotten. Stuermer navigated while Jap drove and in the bitter cold both were thankful that the old Citroën's heater worked. Now and again Stuermer thought of the men in the open back – but at least they could sleep and huddle together for warmth. He and Jap had to stay awake throughout the endless night, eyes fixed on the instruments.

They stopped in a small wadi at dawn, ate a hasty breakfast and then, camouflaging the truck the best they could with a few pieces of camel thorn that they had left from their cooking fires, they flung themselves under it and fell into a dreamless sleep.

Most of them awoke in the afternoon and moaned at the impact of that tremendous heat which seemed to dry up their very blood, cursing the searingly hot air under the truck, which offered no real respite.

Just before dark, they set off again on another long night in the freezing cold, the engine screaming shrilly in protest as, kilometre after kilometre, Jap forced it northwards. This second night, however, was not as tranquil as the first. Time and time again the men in the cab spotted spurts of scarlet flame far to the north, stabbing the velvet night before vanishing again as mysteriously as they had appeared; and it was a long time before they realized what they were.

'Aeroplane exhausts, that's what they are,' Ox-Jo announced confidently. 'Seen their like before at *Furstenfeldbruck* Air Field last year when I was on leave. I was knocking off a bit of gash – er, excuse me Major Greul – I was courting a young lady around that way and when we were – er – having a little chat with the blackout curtains drawn back, I could see the night fighters practising. They made the same flashes in the sky.'

Stuermer absorbed the information thoughtfully for a few moments. 'Then we must be getting pretty close to their fields now,' he concluded. 'The Americans' I mean. But why are they exercising at night? They're committed to daylight bombing.'

It was Greul who came up with the answer this time. 'It can mean only one thing, sir. They are exercising at night so that our listening posts in Greece and Italy are caught off guard.'

'How do you mean?'

'Well, normally, sir, just before a bombing raid, there's an increase in radio traffic, morse signals and the like as the operators practise the new set of codes and signals in formation. Now, as the Amis usually bomb by day, our people in signals detection won't be on the lookout for their signals at this time of night. That means—'

Stuermer beat him to it. 'That the Americans are getting ready to raid Ploesti soon!' he said excitedly.

'Exactly, sir,' Greul agreed staring to the north as the night sky was illuminated yet once again by a faint spurt of scarlet. 'It can only be a matter of days now before they set off on their mission.' He frowned, as if he had suddenly become aware of the full significance of his own words. 'Time is running out for Stormtroop Edelweiss . . .'

Just before dawn that day they started to enter a rocky defile. Soon they were creeping along at a snail's pace, dwarfed by the steep limestone cliffs on both sides which reached upwards like a series of gigantic steps.

Ox-Jo, who was driving now, nudged a sleepy Jap and said, 'All right, ape-shit, out you go and give me directions. There's a drop of fifty metres to my right and it might bring back your migraine if we fall down there.'

Jap was out of the door and hurrying to the front of the big truck in a flash.

Ox-Jo, tensed behind the wheel, had eyes for nothing but Jap's silent figure outlined against the lightening desert sky, as he directed the truck in and out of the rough trail that led through the depression, his nostrils increasingly aware of an ever stronger smell of moist rotting grass.

'It's an oasis coming up,' Stuermer whispered to Greul, not wishing to distract the sweating NCO hunched over the wheel. 'That's causing the stink.'

A few minutes later he was proved right. Jap directed Ox-Jo round a corner and there, outlined in the first pink light of the new day, was a mud village perched high on the top of a curiously shaped, white rock formation that rose straight into the sky like a giant mushroom.

Jap hit the brakes, immediately, so that they were still half-concealed by the rocks alongside the track and flashed Stuermer an inquiring look.

By way of answer, Stuermer slapped his hand hard three times on the back of the cab. It was the signal for an immediate stand-to, and almost immediately the Storm-troop men began to roll over the side, weapons at the ready.

While they crouched there on either side of the rocky track, Stuermer and Greul focused their glasses on the hill-top village. Unlike the tented camp of the nomadic Tuaregs, this was obviously a permanent settlement. The circle of huts, grouped around what appeared to be a primitive mosque, were made of baked mud and roofed with palm fronds. Here and there, they saw the lazy trails of smoke rising from the huts. So the huts had permanent fire-places.

Stuermer lowered his glasses and looked at Greul. 'What do you make of it, Major?' he asked, trying to collect his own thoughts, realizing already that the hill-top village dominated the whole flat desert around for many kilometres. Nothing could pass it during daylight hours without being seen from that height.

'Well, sir, they are obviously not nomads like the usual desert Arab. Those are permanent dwellings, however primitive, and there is a mosque, too, as you can see.'

Stuermer nodded. 'Yes, that is my thinking, too.' For a moment or two, he frowned as he considered what to do next. According to his calculations the American airfields could not be more than a few hours away. If they set off now, they would probably reach them by early afternoon; but where would they lie up till dark which was when they had planned to begin their great sabotage operation? Even the Americans, as careless as they were in such matters, would have security patrols out, checking the perimeters of their fields. Out there in the desert, they would stick out like sore thumbs in daylight.

'Greul,' he said suddenly, his mind made up, 'we shall take that village. It will make an ideal base of operations. We'll spend the day there, sally forth tonight, carry out our task and then *come back* and lie up there until the heat is off. Then we'll have to contact Berlin and get ourselves picked up, either by sub or high-speed motor launch.'

'*Ausgezeichnet*,' Greul answered, 'an excellent idea, sir, if I may be allowed to say so?'

'You may,' Stuermer said ironically.

But as usual irony was wasted on the tall hard-faced Major. 'What's the drill, sir?' he snapped.

Stuermer indicated the dusty winding trail that led up to the mud village. 'There's no reason to make an obvious military operation of the business. The truck is a civilian model and we are dressed in civilian clothes. We shall drive in casually, and take it from there. Why should the natives take us for anything else but civilians?'

'And if there are enemy troops up there?'

'Then, my dear Greul, we better be prepared to fight like hell.' Stuermer waved a hand at Greul's dirty white robe. 'Because we're in civvies and it will not have escaped your notice that when soldiers dressed in civilian clothes are captured, they are usually shot against the nearest wall – *as spies*!'

Major Greul blanched slightly under his tan. 'I take your point, sir. We must take all precautions.'

'That we must, Greul, that we must,' Stuermer replied and this time there was no irony in his voice.

They rattled and bumped their way up the steep trail around the hill, as the rays of the sun flushed the desert floor a warm red hue. It was going to be another very hot day. To the north the brilliant blue sky was streaked with white vapour trails as the Americans took to the air yet once again, practising for the great day. The sight reminded Stuermer anew of the urgency of their mission and he clutched the machine-pistol concealed on his lap a little more tightly, hoping against hope that they would encounter no trouble in the village. He wanted to get on with their impossible task and be rid of this cruel country for good.

Now they were rolling over coarse grass with flakes of encrusted salt gleaming white between the tufts. Here and there, little black goats tethered under the rustling palms cropped the grass listlessly, raising their heads to stare blankly at the passing vehicle for a moment before resuming their eating. Jap nudged Ox-Jo. 'One or two of them'd make a nice change from Old Man, Ox, eh? Roasted on a spit, seasoned with a bit of wild garlic and—'

'Be quiet!' Stuermer snapped and the very next moment regretted his harshness. The strain was beginning to tell. He was losing his nerve.

In a heavy silence, broken only by the noises of the engine labouring up the steep track in first gear, they swung round the last bend and saw the village spread out in front of them.

Ox-Jo stopped without orders under the cover of a

clump of palms, while the men in the cab furtively surveyed the place like a group of thieves.

There was little to see. It was almost as if the village was still asleep, though the smoke coming from the palm-leaf roofs indicated that it wasn't. A skinny dog mooched among the trash of the dirt road. A couple of chickens picked idly for corn. And an Arab, huddled under a palm tree, lay snoring.

Stuermer looked at Greul. The latter nodded, and said, 'Looks safe enough to me, sir.'

'All right, but we'll take no chances. Ox, take the vehicle in slowly. Jap here will give you cover if there's any trouble. We'll come in on both sides of the track, round the back of those huts – just in case.'

'Yessir. No problem,' Ox said, placing a stick grenade with pull-string ready and dangling on the dashboard in front of him. Hurriedly Stuermer took command of the troopers to the right of the track, while Greul did the same with those on the left. With a curt nod, he indicated they should start forward.

Tense, nerves jingling a little, bodies bent slightly forward as always on such occasions, the Edelweiss men advanced on the silent village, their boots making no noise in the thick white dust.

There was no noise now, save the rumble of the Citroën's engine and the braying of a donkey somewhere on the other side of the village.

Suddenly, the men halted without command, their damp forefingers curling round their triggers apprehensively. A figure had appeared at the door of the nearest hut, raising his head to the sky and yawning luxuriously like a man who had just enjoyed a good sleep – he was dressed in a uniform!

He turned and saw the robed troopers crouched under the palms, but no fear appeared on his handsome, cunning face. '*M'ah Salama y'ah Effendi*,' he began in Arabic and then stopped suddenly, as he realized that these were not Arabs but white men.

Stuermer studied the man's uniform. He wore the oversized shorts of the British Army and his shirt bore the kind of regimental flash that the Tommies used, too. But over the left-hand pocket there was a lighter patch, where had once been sewn the eagle and swastika of the Greater German Army. He frowned. What would a British soldier be doing in this remote village? he asked himself, his bewilderment growing.

'Who are you?' Stuermer asked abruptly in German, knowing whoever the stranger was and whatever he was doing here, he, Stuermer, had the drop on him – for the time being at least.

He was not prepared for the bare-headed soldier's reaction. For he snapped to attention in the German fashion, finger-tips stretched down the seams of his overlong shorts, head tilted in the air, body rigid, and barked: '*Sergeant Hannemann of the Free German Army reporting, SIR!*'

EIGHT

'The Free German Army?' Stuermer echoed incredulously, eyeing the handsome young soldier, still standing rigidly to attention in spite of the flies crawling over his sweating face. 'What in three devils' name is that? Oh, for God's sake, stand at ease, man!'

'Thank you, sir.' Sergeant Hannemann of the Free German Army thrust out his right foot to the at ease position, placed his hands behind his back as regulations prescribed, and smiling up at Stuermer with those winning blue eyes of his, said, 'There are a dozen of us who got left behind by – er – our officers when they left us somewhat – er – hurriedly.'

Greul flushed angrily, but he was too amazed by Hannemann to do more than that.

'We had to fend for ourselves because we didn't want to go into the bag, so we formed our own Army, just like all the rest of them did.'

Stuermer shook his head, his bewilderment increasing. 'The rest of them? Who are the rest of them?' he snapped. Hannemann was in no way put out by Stuermer's angry bark. In spite of his scrupulous observation of military courtesies, he was obviously not a man particularly impressed by rank. 'Oh,' he declared airily, 'the Tommies, the Macaronies, the Greeks, the Aussies, oh, the whole shower of 'em out here in the desert who went over the hill because they had a noseful of their own particular army.'

'You mean *deserters*, Sergeant?' Greul barked, recovering a little.

'That's right, sir,' Hannemann said cheerfully. 'You see, it's a long way back to the big cities, the Gippo places like

Cairo and Alex, so they just buggered off into the blue – excuse me, the desert to you, sir – and lived off the land.'

'Lived off the land?' Stuermer echoed.

'Yessir. There are abandoned supply dumps everywhere in the blue, with Aussie bully and Tommy stew, Eyetie wine, Scotch whisky, everything the heart desires and if they want cancer sticks, they just knock off a supply truck. The only thing there ain't is – er – women.' He looked coyly at his highly polished British boots and an admiring Ox-Jo said warmly, 'That you can say agen, mate!'

'And you did the same?' Stuermer queried.

'Yessir. We decided we'd play the same game and, so far, nobody's tumbled to us. When we bump into those Ami flyboys over there, which we occasionally do, they take us for a genuine military outfit. The Americans aren't too swift in the upper storey – fortunately.'

Stuermer sucked his teeth and stared at the men coming from within the hut, all dressed in a similar fashion to Hannemann, the uniforms neat, their hair cropped short in the military fashion. Something about them irritated him. They were soldierly, each of them saluting with rigid precision as they lined up in front of him and Stormtroop Edelweiss, and respectful; yet there was something about their eyes which he didn't like. But he was too tired to pursue the matter. 'And the natives?' he asked, changing the subject.

'The nig-nogs?' Hannemann said airily. 'Oh, they're all right. We've got them tamed. They do as we say 'cos they know we're the providers of easy loot – and that's all that concerns yer average nig-nog.' With a sneer he made the gesture of swiping something and placing it behind his back. 'That's all that concerns them.'

'They're safe, are they?' Greul inquired urgently. 'I mean they won't betray the—' He stopped short.

Hannemann lowered his gaze so that the two officers could not see the sudden change of expression in his eyes. 'Safe as houses, gentlemen. But may I be as bold to ask where you have come from and what your purpose is? I mean, gentlemen, I can tell you aren't from the old *Afrika Korps*. So if I may—'

'You may not,' Stuermer cut him off curtly. 'Now what about providing some hot food for my chaps, since you seem to be so well supplied, and giving us somewhere where we can get our heads down for a while. We've been travelling a long time.'

Sergeant Hannemann of the Free German Army threw up his hands in a theatrical gesture that Stuermer knew instinctively was fake. 'What am I thinking about, gentlemen? Please forgive me. Kurt – and you Klaus,' he snapped at the other members of his strange force. 'Don't stand there like a fart waiting to hit the shithouse wall. Rustle up some grub for the gentlemen. Come on now. *Dalli . . . dalli*. Time's money, you know,' and his winning eyes narrowed suddenly into a cunning leer, as if he really believed that old cliché.

'What do you think, Hanni?' Kurt asked as the members of the Free German Army huddled under a palm and listened to the snores of the new arrivals.

They had fed them beans and roasted goat-meat, washed down with large quantities of looted British whisky. Now the men of Edelweiss were sunk, or so it appeared, in an exhausted, drunken sleep.

'Don't know,' Hannemann replied laconically, deep in thought, trying to make out who his unexpected visitors were and why they were here. As always he had an eye on the main chance, and somehow he suspected that they endangered his happy little life out of the war in this remote oasis.

Sergeant Hannemann had not been abandoned by his officers, as he had told Stuermer. Instead, he had abandoned them – exactly one year before the great debacle of the *Afrika Korps* which had led to its surrender in North Africa.

In the summer of 1942 while on leave he had pulled his old trick of substituting officer's stars for those of a non-commissioned officer. With their help he had managed to get a ride to Derna on the coast, a place in the officers' hostel there and the kind of food and drink that Rommel reserved for his officers corps. Unfortunately, he had decided that same night to enjoy another privilege reserved strictly for officers and gentlemen; he had visited Derna's Officers' brothel. He had passed the chaindog[1] on guard outside successfully, had bluffed his way past the *madame* and was on his way up the stairs to the girls, already excited by the sound of energetically squeaking bed springs, when suddenly he had been confronted by the angry red face of his own CO.

Words like 'outright scandal' . . . court-martial . . . punishment battalion at the front . . .' had flown. And for once in his charmed young life, Sergeant Hannemann, always the winner, never the loser, had lost his head. He had drawn the knife he always kept concealed in the back pocket of his shorts and stabbed his CO three times in the chest.

The Colonel had collapsed and died there at his feet almost before he had realized what he had done. So Hannemann had fled blindly out into the coastal city and from thence deep into the desert, hearing the police whistles and sirens dying away behind him. From that time onwards, as the Tommies pushed the *Afrika Korps* ever westwards until finally what was left of it had surrendered to Montgomery, Sergeant Hannemann had lived on his wits, hijacking solitary trucks, looting abandoned depots, sneak-thieving from stores. Until, finally, he had collected others of the same ilk – petty thieves, deserters and murderers – under his own command and together they had taken over the native village, using the terrified natives little better than slaves, even taking their women when the need arose.

Now, the presence of these strangers in civilian dress who had appeared so mysteriously out of nowhere, months

[1] Military policeman.

after the last armed German soldier had long disappeared from North Africa, worried him a great deal.

They were fighting men, all right. He could see that. They were there on some mission. That he knew, also. The question was – would their mission, whatever it was, endanger the nice little set-up he had going here? For Sergeant Hannemann had plans. Unknown to the others, who, in his opinion, were born losers who would never survive the war anyway, he was already preparing for *his* post-war career. Two kilometres from where he now sat, he had buried the 'war chest' of a Bavarian tank regiment: a small metal case of tiny gold bars with which the Bavarians had been supplied to pay off the natives in an emergency. With it, once the war ended, he intended to buy himself a passage on a ship to South Africa, far away from a dying Europe; for he had no illusions about what was going to happen to the old continent once the war was finished. And just when he had finally gotten himself a nice little set-up, these strangers had come along, bringing back conveniently forgotten memories of the Greater German *Wehrmacht* and the war.

'I think, fellers,' he announced finally, 'we've got to do something about them?' he jerked a thumb at the men snoring under the shade of the palms, while the little swollen native boys idly fanned the flies away from their sweat-glazed faces.

'What exactly?' Kurt, the rapist and deserter, asked.

Hannemann sucked his excellent teeth thoughtfully. 'Well, my guess is that they're here on account of the Amis up there to the north. So far they've left us in peace. I scratch you and you scratch me, that's the way the Americans seem to work. But,' he held up his forefinger in warning, 'things might change if this gang here gets up to any nasty tricks.' There was low rumble of agreement from his listeners. 'So, I say,' Hannemann continued, selecting his words with care, 'that the Amis ought to be told about them.'

One or two of his listeners looked shocked. There was a

gasp, and VD, the little bespectacled corporal who had been an orderly in Benghazi's Venereal Disease Hospital, protested. 'I say, Hanni, that's going a bit far, ain't it – they are German, too, you know!'

But Kurt, the rapist, represented the main opinion among the members of the Free German Army. 'You mean shop 'em to the Amis, Hanni?' he snapped, laying it on the line.

'Yes.'

Kurt considered for a few moments. 'Got to be careful, though, Hanni. The Amis might start asking awkward questions about us, too, yer know.'

'I do,' Hannemann smiled, but his cunning eye didn't light up. 'What we got the nig-nogs for, eh?'

'Of course!' Kurt agreed. 'Let them do the palaver with the Amis, that way we're out of it.'

'So this is the way we're gonna do it, comrades,' Hannemann decided, lowering his voice so that the others had to lean forward to hear his words.

Behind the plotters, the exhausted troopers of Stormtroop Edelweiss snored on, unaware that their fate and perhaps that of Germany itself was being decided by a handful of murderers, rapists and petty thieves . . .

BOOK THREE

'Then let each man turn straight to the front, come death, come life—
That's how war and battle kiss and prattle.'

The Iliad

ONE

Leutnant von Ernst ducked instinctively as the great silver plane came hurtling downwards at the target, coughing and choking as the dust cloud enveloped him, deafened by the tremendous roar of the plane's four engines. Then the Liberator was gone, leaving the practice bombs smoking right in the centre of the circular target.

He wiped the dust from his eyes and, raising his binoculars once more, focused them again on the oddly disparate pair moving steadily across the desert towards the tented American camps.

For days now he had been watching the place and its environs, hoping each new morning, as he crept out of the 'nest', shaking Percy's skeletal hand as was his custom, that it was for the last time and that soon he would be reunited with his fellow countrymen. But each evening he had returned, sadly, to his hiding place, his hopes dashed – for there had been no sign of the men he was anxiously expecting to appear from the south.

Now, however, his hopes were raised. The pair of them out there in the dunes could well be some sort of recce party: an Arab leading a man in uniform on a camel, both pausing frequently to observe the sprawling tented camp as if they were uneasy, on edge. Von Ernst repressed his mounting excitement and desire to rush out and declare himself to them. Instead, he remained crouched in his hiding place watching their every move as they began to approach the camp to the right of the bombing range. Soon, he told himself, they would stop and find a suitable position to observe the place, if they were really the men from the missing glider.

But the two lone figures did not do what von Ernst

expected them to do. Admittedly, they both paused near a wrecked tank, but instead of taking up positions there to observe the Americans, as von Ernst anticipated, the white man slipped from his camel, settled himself behind the tank in its shade with his rifle at the ready and then snapped some order at the Arab. The latter mounted the kneeling beast reluctantly and seemed hesitant to go on. The white man waved his weapon threateningly at the robed native, who, digging his stick into the beast's neck, trotted away in the direction of the camp.

At that very moment another bomber came zooming in at fifty metres' height, blotting out the sun for an instant, releasing wooden bombs, trailing smoke flares, from its fat silver belly before roaring up once again into the bright blue sky. But the white man, crouched in the shade of the tank, did not even look up; his gaze was concentrated exclusively on the lone rider heading for the white-painted guardhouse of the main camp. Von Ernst frowned. Something strange was going on, something very strange indeed.

'Holy cow, Bull!' Killer Kane bellowed over the roar of yet another triumphant Liberator buzzing the camp and setting the tents off flapping violently in its prop wash. 'What did you say?'

Captain Bull Bulcombe beamed hugely, happy to be the centre of attraction, as Kane's staff officers crowded around him to hear his news. 'An Ar-ab has just reported in that there are some Krauts back there in the desert about to attempt to sabotage the mission. They'll be heading this way – probably – tonight.'

Killer Kane smote his forehead angrily. 'Now that's just real swell,' he exclaimed. 'Forty-eight hours to Tidal Wave – as if that ain't headache enough – and now a bunch of Kraut saboteurs are going to hit us! Do you know just how big our perimeter is? With nary a guardpost in its whole length! Oh, my aching back, what a mess!'

Bull Bulcombe's beam did not change. He seemed to be

totally unaffected by his CO's reaction. 'I've got a plan, sir, if it's OK with you.'

Killer Kane did not seem to be listening. Yesterday morning there had been a full-dress rehearsal for the big raid, the Liberators using live bombs for the first time. It had been a spectacular success, with the Liberators' squadrons stretching five miles wide, wing-tip to wing-tip, obliterating the facsimile target within two minutes flat. The wildly elated aircrews had finished with an unauthorized buzz of the camp, clipping the tops from the palms and tearing up the tents by the pegs with their massed prop-wash. Kane had not objected later. He, too, had felt the same elation, his days of doubt and gloom vanished at last. That day he had seen what he believed to be the poised strength of the finest aerial task force in the world and he had known they would succeed. They *would* wipe out Ploesti. Now big, loud-mouthed Bulcombe came blundering in, spoiling everything with his talk of German saboteurs. For even if these unknown Krauts existed only in the imagination of some goddam Arab out for *baksheesh*, it did mean that the locals knew about Tidal Wave; and if the locals knew, it could well indicate that the Krauts across in Europe did, too.

'Where is this damned Arab of yours, Bull?' he interrupted the big Captain's flow of words. 'Get him in here at double time. Pronto!'

'Yessir,' Bull said. 'In a brace of shakes, sir.'

'Oh, for crying out loud, Bull, don't make a production of it – get him in!'

But when Captain Bulcombe returned, he was still alone, a puzzled frown creasing his narrow brow.

Kane looked up at him from the paper-littered desk. 'So where's the Arab?' he demanded.

Bulcombe shrugged a little helplessly. 'Don't know, sir. I asked the MP to keep an eye on him, but he had to go and take a piss and when he came back, the nigger had done a bunk.'

Kane shook his head. 'Christ on a crutch, Bull, you

certainly do pull 'em.' First you have an Arab telling ya that the Krauts are gonna sabotage the base – and then you don't have him.'

'But sir, he existed all right. The MPs can vouch for that.'

'And he told them the same story he told you?'

'No sir,' Bull Bulcombe answered a little helplessly. 'He wanted to tell what he knew to an officer only. You know these niggers? They always think somebody's gonna cheat them of their dash. So he wouldn't speak till he saw an officer – me.'

Kane pursed his lips. 'You believed him?'

'One hundred per cent. He didn't look the type capable of making up a story like that.'

'I see.' Killer Kane made his decision. ' 'Kay, Bull, this is what we're gonna do. I'll put the base on security alert, not that that will help much. This place is wide-open. You,' he pointed a finger almost accusingly at the big, broad-shouldered pilot, as if it were his fault that this new burden had been placed on his shoulders, 'will take the reserve and stand-down crews, let's say three of them. That's about all I can spare. Go over to the Motor Pool and get yourselves some jeeps and go looking for this Arab. When you find him, Bull, get *exact* - and I repeat, *exact* – details of these Kraut saboteurs, if they exist,' he added, his voice lowered a little.

Bull Bulcombe looked down at his CO in dismay. 'But sir,' he protested. 'It might take me a couple of days to find him again in that desert out there and in forty-eight hours we fly the mission. Have a heart, sir, I don't want to miss the op, not after all this practice.' He licked his lips, his voice full of pleading.

Killer Kane picked up his fountain pen and looked down at the papers scattered in front of him on the desk once more. 'Tough titty, Bull,' he said unfeelingly. 'Why don't you take it up with the chaplain one of these days? Now on your way, buddy.'

Helplessly Bull touched his hand to his forehead in

salute and stumbled out of the hot little office into the glare of the midday sun. Suddenly, he realized in his search for personal glory he had put his foot in it and if he weren't very careful, he'd miss Tidal Wave. As the CO had said, it was very tough titty indeed. And then his old resolve and aggressive determination started to function once more, and, seeing Shorty Perkins and the Prof lounging in the shade opposite waiting for him, he cried with new energy, 'Hey, you two lugs, let's get on the stick!'

'Where we going?' Shorty cried back.

'To the Motor Pool to get some jeeps and then we're gonna round up some of the guys!'

'But why, Bull?' the Prof asked puzzled.

' 'Cos, Killer's allowed us to go off hunting for the day – and it ain't deer we're looking for. Cut the cackle and let's get on with it. Move yer butts!' And with that, in spite of the crippling heat, Bull Bulcombe was running powerfully across the sand towards the Motor Pool, with a helpless Prof and Shorty Perkins stumbling after him.

Thirty minutes later, von Ernst, who had watched the disappearance of the Arab and the lone white man into the desert and was now preparing to follow them, was surprised by the sight of the six jeeps, laden with shouting American airmen, leaving the camp. Rumbling along in low gear, the lead jeep, directed by a tall brutal-looking American, who von Ernst recognized after a few moments as the one who had tortured the seaplane crewman, started to follow the tracks made by the camel in the sand.

Von Ernst clubbed his fist and struck the sand excitedly. It had to be it, he told himself. The whole thing tied up somehow – exactly how he didn't know. But that strange couple and the sudden appearance of these loud noisy Americans, now slowly moving past his hiding place following the camel's heavy marks, were linked to the missing glidermen. They had to be. It was the only explanation.

The officer made a decision. He waited till the jeep convoy was past, then he checked his water bottle. It was full, sufficient water to last him forty-eight hours, if he was careful. In the pocket of his robe he had a wad of pressed dates and a tin of British corned beef, food enough for the same period of time. And concealed under the dirty white cotton sheet, he could feel the comforting hardness of his American grease-gun. He felt prepared for anything.

He smiled at the backs of the disappearing Americans and said aloud, 'Don't go too fast, comrades. Have a little pity on a wounded soldier.' Then shouldering his water bottle, he started to limp after them, following their tracks now in the sand.

All decisions had now been made. The time for action had arrived.

TWO

It was nearly dusk. On the horizon the sun had become a blood-red ball, hovering there and flushing the desert a warm pink. Soon it would make its usual dramatic departure, leaving the observers blinking and momentarily blinded in the sudden abrupt darkness.

Over at the Citroën Ox-Jo and Jap made their final checks, belching happily as they pottered around, for Hannemann and his Arabs had served them an excellent evening meal of medami, onions, sliced radish and freshly baked unleavened bread, washed down with looted Italian red wine. It would be enough to last them until their mission was well completed, Stuermer could not help but think, as he strolled about the camp, checking that his troopers were ready to move off as soon as it was dark, followed by the over-solicitous Hannemann, who kept rubbing his hands like some third-class head waiter out for a big tip.

Stuermer paused for a few moments and watched, as each trooper filed by Major Greul to receive his slap of plastic explosive and handful of time pencils, the air suddenly full of the stink of almonds which came from the British-made explosive.

At his side, Hannemann frowned abruptly. He recognized the time pencils, the usual device to set off the explosive in any sabotage operation, but the slabs of pliable brown material, which looked for all the world like the plasticine used in schools for modelling, were new to him.

Stuermer caught the look out of the corner of his eyes, but he did not enlighten the handsome young NCO. He hadn't quite made up his mind about Hannemann. The man was exceedingly pleasant and helpful, yet the members of his Free German Army were obviously scum. Deceit was written all over their faces; he wouldn't trust one of them. It was obvious they were sitting out the war here in this remote oasis, living off what they could steal, and were in no way inclined to return to the lethal business of fighting.

Hannemann was different. All the same he had not once asked about their mission, or indeed where and how they had gotten here. For such an intelligent, winning man, that in itself was strange.

Stuermer forgot the matter as Ox-Jo swung the starting handle of the Citroën and, after a few throaty grunts, it burst into noisy life sending the Arabs' dusty chickens scuttling for cover. He turned to the NCO. 'Sergeant Hannemann.'

Hanneman snapped to attention, as if he were back on some peacetime parade ground. 'Sir?' he barked.

'We shall be moving out in a few moments, Hannemann,' Stuermer began and then after a moment's hesitation took a chance, wondering as he did so what kind of reaction he would get from the NCO. 'However, it could be that we might return in due course.' Hannemann's handsome face showed no reaction whatsoever. Stuermer tested him further. 'There might be trouble,' he added in a soft voice, as the heavily armed and rested troopers started to pile into the truck.

Hannemann's Adam's apple moved up and down his skinny throat. Stuermer noted the involuntary gesture. The NCO was worried. 'I see, sir,' he said after a moment and then, recovering himself, added, 'I can assure you we will await your return, sir, whatever the trouble. You can rely on the men of the Free German Army.'

Suddenly, with the finality of a vision, Stuermer knew that the handsome man facing him was up to something. Lowering his gaze so that the other man could not see the look in his eyes, he said, 'We shall be heading in the general direction of Derna. I reckon that it might take us two days to get there. If we do return, you can expect us in about four to five days from now.'

'Yessir,' Hannemann replied with no emotion in his voice.

Stuermer looked up and saw that the other man knew he was lying. Hanneman knew their objective, all right, and he had known from the very minute they had entered his camp.

Stuermer nodded to Greul. The Major walked over to the truck and, while Stuermer kept Hannemann occupied, stole quickly away down the track into the ever growing shadows, and as the big Citroën lumbered past him down the trail and halted to wait for the two officers, he quickly scattered the little explosive devices across the trail. If anyone followed them tonight, they would be in for an unpleasant surprise. Then as Stuermer answered Hannemann's immaculate salute and strode off, Greul clambered into the cab of the truck. A minute later Stuermer joined him. 'All right?' he queried, as Ox-Jo rammed home first gear and the dust-covered truck started to move forward once more.

'All right, sir.'

'Good.' Stuermer settled back in the cab and closed his eyes, though he knew he would be unable to sleep; there were too many problems racing through his troubled mind. They were on the way on the last stage of their journey.

Behind them Hannemann waved as he watched the ancient vehicle rumble round a bend in the trail and said cynically out of the side of his mouth to the corporal known as 'VD'. 'Goodbye dum-dums . . . go and die for Folk, Fatherland and Führer . . .'

'Hold it . . . *I say, hold it there, buster!*' Bull Bulcombe called over the noise of the jeep's motor, circling round so that the headlights fell on the Arab leading the camel and bathed him and the white man on it in its icy white light. The others in the jeep raised their Tommy guns.

Kurt the rapist panicked. In the same moment that the

terrified Arab forced the camel to kneel, he flung himself from the hump and reached for his pistol.

Instinctively, the Prof pressed the trigger of his Tommy gun. The weapon chattered into violent activity. Kurt screamed, flinging up his arms crazily, as the burst ripped along his chest and the blood spurted out from half a dozen smoking holes. He staggered a few paces, his legs giving way beneath him like those of a newly born foal; then he fell flat on his face, twitched a couple of times and died, watched by an open-mouthed Prof, who had never killed a man before.

But Bulcombe had no time for the dead German. Turning the body over and satisfying himself that he was dead, he pulled away his boot to let him fall back on his face once more and turned to the Arab who had gone down on his knees, his hands raised in the classic pose of supplication. Bull knocked the skinny brown arms away and rasped, ' 'Kay, don't try to shit me with that nigger talk! You spoke pretty damn fine American the last time you talked to me. Now what gives?'

Still the Arab wailed something in his own tongue, his eyes large and white in his dark, hook-nosed face. Bull lost all patience. He grabbed the man by the front of his dirty robe. 'Now come on, buddy, don't give me that crap! Where are them Krauts you told me about? Now come on, spit it out, or brother, you're gonna be lacking a set of front teeth in one second flat.'

Whether the terrified native understood Bulcombe's words was doubtful. But the big American's tone sufficed. He pointed one trembling hand at the tall mushroom-shaped hill behind, outlined a stark black against the warm velvet of the night sky, and muttered something in Arabic, adding, 'Germans . . . many Germans . . . there . . . on hill.'

Bull let go of him and beamed at the others, a self-satisfied smile on his big face. 'Didn't I tell you guys. There are Krauts out there after all. You can't make a dummy out of old Bull Bulcombe.'

'Okay, Bull, don't cream yer skivvies,' the Prof said in disgust, looking at the silent hill with some apprehension. 'What we gonna do about it? Shouldn't we high-tail it outa here and report in to Killer?'

'Yeah,' Shorty Perkins and half a dozen of the others agreed, and somebody said, 'Killer can contact the doughs and let them take care of the Krauts. We ain't trained for that kind of thing.'

Bull grinned back at their protesting faces. 'Jesus H, what a bunch of nervous Nellies you guys are! We've got these cannon,' he slapped his big paw against the round barrel of the Tommy gun, 'and we've got surprise on our side. The Kraut has yet to be born who can take old Bull Bulcombe. Now come on, put some pepper in yer pants. Let's get going.' He grabbed the Arab and thrust him bodily into the back of the lead jeep. 'Okay, nigger, lead us to them – and brother, if you're lying, I'm gonna have the nuts off'n yer skinny black carcass before you can say Jack Robinson. Right, Prof, just don't sit there. Hit that gas pedal, and let's—' He stopped in mid-sentence.

'What is it, Bull?' the Prof quavered, suddenly alarmed by the look on the big pilot's face.

'That,' Bull said, swallowing hard and pointing to the gloom, from which was emerging a huge, bull-nosed vehicle, its engine roaring mightily. 'What the Sam Hill is it? It looks as if it just came outa the goddam Ark!'

'*Amis!*' Ox-Jo yelled in that same instant, spotting the little column of jeeps and automatically swerving to the right, as the first wild burst of tracer cut the darkness, missing the truck by metres.

Stuermer slapped his palm hard on the back of the cab, and flung himself out of the still moving vehicle, rolling over in the sand and coming round firing, while behind him the men of Edelweiss dropped expertly into the sand and started doing the same.

Almost immediately, a wild fire fight broke out with the

red, white and green tracer zipping back and forth in crazy frenetic anger.

Ox-Jo, still sitting behind the wheel next to Jap said angrily, above the snap and crackle of the small arms battle, 'Stuff this for a tale, apeturd!' Furiously he rammed home first gear.

'What yer gonna do, Ox?' his companion yelled as he swung the big wheel round.

'What d'yer think, you perverted banana-sucker. I'm gonna charge them!' Ox-Jo roared and let out the clutch.

'*Charge them!*' Jap cried in alarm, as the truck lurched forward abruptly flinging him against the back of the cab. 'You ain't got all yer cups in yer cupboard, man—'

'Hell,' Ox interrupted, hunched intently over the big wheel, the tracer rushing to meet them like deadly hailstones, 'they're not soldiers. They're just Ami flyboys. Hold on to yer knickers, here we go!'

The windscreen shattered and showered them with broken glass. Ox roared angrily. Freeing one hand, he cleared the glass away, the blood gushing unheeded from his lacerated knuckles. Next to him, Jap smashed the rest away with the butt of his Schmeisser. He thrust through the muzzle and pressed the trigger.

'That's the stuff to give the troops!' Ox yelled enthusiastically, as they drew ever closer to the jeeps, bolting and lurching across the uneven desert floor, a huge wake of sand flying behind them, the slugs howling noisily off the Citroën's sides. 'We'll show them egg-and-bacon-for-breakfast flyboys what real soldiers are! Ready for boarding, cap'n! *NOW!*'

At forty kilometres an hour, he smashed the bonnet of the big old truck right into the side of the leading jeep. The bonnet crumpled like a banana-skin as the jeep slowly lurched over, flinging out the screaming, terrified airmen.

Jap dived through the door which had suddenly swung open, his machine-pistol hissing furiously at a 1,000 slugs a minute. An American loomed up at his front and went down screaming the next moment, his face dripping down on to his chest like molten red wax. Another sat down abruptly, holding his guts which slid out of his ripped open stomach like a grey steaming snake, with an almost apologetic grin on his ashen face.

A big man reached in the cab and pulled out Ox who sat behind his shattered wheel, momentarily in a daze. Suddenly Ox woke up to his danger. 'Get yer dirty Ami paws off'n me!' he yelled in red-eyed fury. He broke the American's hold on his dirty robe and brought his knee up sharply. It connected with Bull Bulcombe's chin. He reeled back, yelping in agony and sat down in a daze. Ox didn't give him time to recover. He raised his cruelly-nailed mountain-boot and smashed it with full force in Bulcombe's dazed face. Something snapped audibly and Bull slammed backwards, blood jetting from his mouth and ears, spitting out teeth before he slid into unconsciousness.

The sight of Bull Bulcombe, their natural leader, going under, took the fight out of the surprised American airmen. Somebody yelled above the crackle of the automatics. 'It's no use guys, they're too many for us . . . I'm giving in!' The speaker dropped his weapon and cautiously stood up behind the jeep where he had taken cover and raised his hands.

The Prof, holding his free hand to his bleeding shoulder, cried in angry protest, 'But you can't give up just like that, Bo, think—' The words died on his lips. Everywhere his comrades were dropping their weapons and raising their hands in surrender.

'Sweet Jesus, what a fucking mess!' the Prof said angrily and dropped his forty-five too, and for once Shorty Perkins could not cross himself at the angry, profane blasphemy. For he, too, had his hands raised in defeat . . .

THREE

'The lousy treacherous bastard!' Ox-Jo snorted and shook his clenched fist at the mushroom-shaped hill. 'Sergeant Hannemann of the Free German Army, I'll have the eggs off'n you with a blunt razor blade yet!'

Stuermer, ignoring the terrible threat, sat pondering the surprising situation they found themselves in since their encounter with the Americans, who now either squatted in the sand with their hands on their heads, or lay wounded and groaning to the rear of the jeeps.

Hannemann had obviously betrayed them to the Americans. The question now was whether he had been in a position to tell the enemy what Stormtroop Edelweiss's objective was. Somehow or other Stuermer thought he had. Why would these airmen be out here in the desert otherwise? In other circumstances, the enemy commanders would have sent in infantry to tackle them.

'What now, sir?' Greul asked a little moodily, as if he too had come to the same conclusion as his CO.

'Don't know exactly,' Stuermer answered, knowing that he had to make up his mind soon; time was running out. Their mission would be impossible to carry out in daylight hours. 'If they have been warned, as I suspect, Greul, and the Amis are waiting for us up there, it could mean the end of Stormtroop Edelweiss.'

'My thinking exactly, sir,' Greul replied, with a frown. 'All the same, to come this far, so many thousands of kilometres, and be cheated when we are so close to the objective—'

'*Meine Herren, darf ich mich vorstellen?*' a cheerful young voice cut into their gloomy ponderings and both of them swung round, their hands reaching for their weapons.

A tall skinny Arab stood there, hands raised in the air, grinning at the surprised looks on their faces. 'Don't shoot,' he said, not losing his grin. 'Don't shoot please, it's the only body I've got – even though it is a trifle shopworn.'

'You're German!' the two of them gasped.

'Yes, may I introduce myself. *Leutnant* von Ernst, late of the *Afrika Korps*.'

'The sleeper!' Stuermer said excitedly, as the 'Arab' started to lower his hands, knowing that he was safe now.

'The sleeper, sir, and glad at last to be awakened by the princess in the fairy tale, though I hasten to say that you, gentlemen, need not kiss me to achieve that end.'

Stuermer smiled. Young von Ernst had a sense of humour, it was obvious. Hastily, he reached in his hip pocket and bringing out the flask of whisky which Hannemann had given him, said, 'Here, pour some of that down your wing-collar and tell us what you know.'

Von Ernst needed no urging and while Ox-Jo and Jap watched him greedily, licking their lips as they did so, he took a deep swig, and then launched into his tale: how he had found the missing glider and had guessed that there was another one somewhere out in the desert, and how he had spotted the renegade German and the Arab contacting the Americans.

'So they *do* know,' Greul said bitterly when he had finished.

Von Ernst nodded. 'Yes, they do, but you must remember the field is a huge sprawling place with no security to speak of. I've been in and out of the place scores of times in my role as shithouse cleaner and general odd-job man. I've never scrubbed so many thunder-boxes since my days as a recruit in 1939!' he added with a grin. 'Even if they are alerted, you can still get in. The problem is that you would be spotted more quickly than you would normally be at night. Obviously they would have patrols wandering about the place and you'd soon be seen in those Arab clothes.'

'But what if we weren't wearing Arab clothing?' Stuermer queried, breaking his own thoughtful silence.

The other two looked at him startled. 'What do you mean, sir?' von Ernst asked.

By way of an answer, Stuermer pointed to the sullen Americans slumped next to the jeeps.

Greul continued to look puzzled, but von Ernst got it at once. 'Of course, *Herr Oberst*, of course! That's a sure way of buying yourself time.' Then his happy grin vanished as quickly as it had appeared. 'But what then, sir? I mean after you've carried out your mission or as much as you can carry out before the Amis tumble to what is going on?'

Again Stuermer had an answer. 'Those Americans are aircrew aren't they? They're all wearing fliers' wings of one kind or another. So, we've got our own air force, haven't we?'

Again von Ernst's happy grin returned and he chortled happily. '*Grosser Gott*, this might well be another von Werra.[1] *Wow!*'

Greul looked from one officer to the other obviously still completely bewildered by the exchange. 'Please,' he said severely, 'will someone tell me what is going on? Von Werra . . . our own air force. What the devil are we talking about?'

Von Ernst turned to him and exploded. 'Talking about? Why, we're going to steal a Liberator, sir!'

'*WHAT!*'

The little convoy of jeeps laden with Americans and what appeared to be Arab workers passed into the field between the white-painted oil drums, which marked the perimeter, without incident. Slowly, strictly observing the 10 mph speed limit posted everywhere, the saboteurs drove on, following von Ernst's whispered instructions. Twice they almost bumped into the Americans, some of them armed, wandering about the field in darkness, but they took no notice of the jeeps. They came parallel with a large blacked out tent from which came the smell of stale beer and faint,

[1] Captain von Werra who attempted to escape from British captivity in 1941 by stealing a Hurricane fighter from a British field.

muffled laughter. 'The sergeants' mess,' von Ernst whispered, 'take the right fork.'

Ox-Jo, now behind the wheel of the lead jeep next to Stuermer, licked his lips, and said thickly, 'What wouldn't I give, sir, to be bellying up to the bar now with a nice big litre of cool suds in my pinkie!'

Stuermer laughed softly and said, 'I promise to buy you a whole brewery full, you rogue, when we get back to Germany.'

'*If*,' Ox-Jo said sourly, but nobody was listening to him. They drove on slowly, pursued by the sounds of '*Pistol-packing mama . . . lay that pistol down . . .*'

Now they started to roll towards the heavy, fat-bellied shapes of the Liberators packed side to side for as far as the eye could see. 'A saboteur's dream,' Stuermer breathed as Greul sitting behind him in the back of the jeep nudged him and said urgently, 'Sentry, two o'clock.'

Stuermer swung his head round quickly. In the faint light he caught the glint of a steel helmet. Greul was right. There was a soldier lounging there, a bayoneted rifle slung over his shoulder. In the same moment that they spotted him, the American spotted them. But his slow turn in the direction of the leading jeep and the almost casual way he unslung his rifle indicated that he was not alarmed. He brought the rifle down and cried, 'Halt – who goes there?', a loud ringing voice.

Ox-Jo clapped his forehead in mock wonder. 'My God, what kind of cardboard soldier is this?'

'Shut up!' Stuermer hissed urgently and, indicating that Ox-Jo should halt, cried back in his best American, 'Friend.'

'Advance one – and be recognized,' the sentry ordered, using the conventional formula. Stuermer grinned at the words and told himself he agreed with Ox-Jo; they were cardboard soldiers. He dropped over the side and advanced upon the waiting sentry. Behind him Jap stole silently into the shadows cast by the nearest Liberator.

'Halt – and be recognized!' the sentry commanded when Stuermer was the regulation six paces away from him.

Obediently, Stuermer did as he was ordered and pretended to be fumbling for his pass while Jap's dark figure detached itself from behind the waiting American.

'Well come on, Captain,' the sentry said, recognizing the twin bars which Stuermer now wore on his shoulders, courtesy Bull Bulcombe, 'let's have it. Colonel Kane is—'

He stopped abruptly as Jap's clubbed fist caught him just where his helmet cleared the nape of his neck. He groaned softly and slumped to the sand with a faint clatter of equipment.

Hurriedly, Jap grabbed the rifle from the unconscious man's nerveless fingers and flung it far into the desert. As an afterthought he bent and arranged the American's hands under his helmet and tucked up his legs as if he were sleeping, saying, 'Good night, sweet prince. May all your dreams be pornographic ones.'

Stuermer grinned. His men were in good heart, in spite of the imminent danger, then his grin vanished as he thought of all the work that lay before Stormtroop Edelweiss this night. 'Come on, Jap. You can give him a goodnight kiss later.'

Those men who were not guarding the sullen Americans now started to drop over the sides of the jeeps everywhere, and hurry towards the line of waiting bombers. A moon had begun to flush the desert night a warm harvest-yellow. Against its light the planes stood out starkly, looking strangely beautiful. In the air they were silver, all-powerful birds; but here those deadly machines, which had taken some thousands of skilled men to create over many months, could be destroyed in a matter of minutes.

Stuermer waited until all his men were collected in front of the long line of Liberators, then he rapped, 'Each man will take four planes. Plant your explosive carefully – and take great care with the time pencils. We want to be out of here before they start exploding. All right, comrades, off you go. I'll give you an hour for this lot. *Dalli . . . dalli . . .*'

Now there was hectic activity the length of the line. The troopers ran to the plane of their choice, clamped the smelly plastic explosive to undercarriage, outer port and starboard engines as they had been shown, before ramming in the time pencil and pulling the wire which activated the detonator. Within minutes they were sweating heavily in spite of the cool breeze now wafting in from the desert and setting the sand off whirling and dancing in excited little flurries about their running feet.

The minutes ticked by rapidly. From the tented camp there came little noise. Occasionally, a bright white beam flickered on and shot skywards, but Stuermer, running and sweating with the rest, reasoned it had something to do with air traffic and not with them. Suddenly, he began to feel confident that they were going to pull off their impossible mission, after all. As he ran from plane to plane, his breath coming in sharp hectic gasps, the sweat streaming down his face, he told himself that the surprise had paid off. The fact that the Americans had been alerted had worked against them.

Then it happened. With startling suddenness the green flare hissed into the velvet glowing sky and hung there for what seemed an age, bathing the faces of the men a sickly ugly hue, as they stared up at it, apprehension written large on their horrified gaze.

'Stand fast everywhere!' Stuermer woke to their danger as over at the camp the headlights began to flick on everywhere and the night stillness was broken by the shrill, nerve-racking screech of an alert siren. 'They've tumbled to us . . . von Ernst, let's be having them now!'

The cries of rage, alarm and fear across at the tents were getting ever louder. There were the first wild hesitant shots, the stutter of a machine-pistol. Red and white tracer stitched the blackness, hurrying towards the stalled troopers at an ever increasing speed.

Searchlights stabbed the night. Hurriedly they were swung round. Icy fingers probed the darkness. A great blinding white light raced across the black night. Stuermer narrowed his eyes to slits.

'Down everyone till the plane's ready! We've got to hold them!' He dropped to the sand, just as a burst of machine-gunfire ripped the air where he had been standing. Next instant he, too, had drawn his machine-pistol and was pumping short controlled bursts right across his front at the dark shapes which were now running towards the trapped saboteurs.

Now it was escape or die . . .

FOUR

The first Americans attacked with reckless courage. They flung their jeeps round in great howling curves, throwing up the dust in a huge yellow cloud, and even before the vehicles had stopped rolling were racing towards the men scattered among the Liberators.

What happened next was not war; it was murder. The aircrewmen had no infantry experience. They bunched and ran straight into the merciless concentrated fire of the Edelweiss veterans. That wall of death stopped them in their tracks. They had never experienced anything like it before. Uncomprehendingly, stunned and confused, they spun round and collapsed like puppets in the hands of an insane puppet-master – most of them dead before they hit the sand.

The wounded, what there were of them, tried to crawl away from that terrible fire, as a second wave of jeeps came bolting and bucking over the desert, their sirens howling, their spots searching out the infiltrators. The Edelweiss troopers didn't give them a chance. They poured a devastating volley of concentrated fire at close range into the wounded. Screaming and yelling piteously, the wounded tried to escape. To no avail. They were hit over and over again, forming solid stacks of dead bodies piled up like cordwood into which the first of the jeeps plunged blindly, scattering their own slaughtered comrades before they realized what they were doing.

Stuermer was experienced enough to know that first terrible volley and the great slaughter it had occasioned would stop the Americans from attacking again just yet. All green troops went to ground and only firm, energetic leadership could persuade them to get up again once they had first seen their own dead. It was always that way. Stuermer had a few minutes' respite. 'Greul,' he yelled above the single shots coming now from the American positions, 'take over for a few moments. I'm going to see how they're getting on with the plane.'

Ducking low and ignoring the crackle of automatic fire that immediately erupted around his flying feet, he pelted for the Liberator in the second line which von Ernst had selected for them. A dark figure came running out of the darkness. He could *smell* he was American. Germans had not washed themselves with perfumed soap like that since 1939. He swung his Schmeisser, muzzle first like a bat. The metal butt struck the unknown American across the face squarely. He could hear the bones snap under the impact of that cruel metal. As the American went down with a howl, Stuermer took a flying kick at his upraised chin. He couldn't afford to take any chances. The American screamed as his spine broke. He lay still. Stuermer raced on.

Panting hard, he grabbed hold of the ladder leading up to the cockpit of the big Liberator that von Ernst had chosen: '*The Wonderful Wizard of Oz*'. With a grunt he pulled himself into the cabin and realized immediately that there was trouble, bad trouble, in the air.

The Americans, their hands clasped to the backs of their necks, stared back defiantly at their captors, while von Ernst threatened them with his pistol.

'What's the matter, von Ernst?' Stuermer asked, taking in the situation at a glance, 'won't they co-operate?'

'No,' von Ernst snarled. 'There are three pilots among them,' he indicated the Americans with the silver wings of pilots on the sun-faded uniforms, 'and all three of them refuse to take the—' The rest of his words were drowned by the rattle of bullets ripping down the length of the fuselage. Jap, who was manning one of the big .50 calibre machine-guns in a side blister, yelled angrily and let forth with a tremendous blast of slugs which shook the whole plane. Stuermer bit his bottom lip. Time was running out.

There were about twenty minutes left before the plastic explosive started to go off. He had calculated that the multiple explosions would so unnerve the Americans that they would get off the ground, at least, unhindered. Now the damned American pilots were refusing to take off. Desperate measures were needed.

He stared along the faces of the three pilots, looking for what he sought – fear in the eyes. The first two were pale and shaken, but undaunted. He knew that it would take too long to work them over enough to make them compliant. The third man was different. A big hulking brute of a fellow, he had a look in his blood-shot eyes that told Stuermer instinctively that he was the weak link in the chain.

He acted. With all his strength, his right hand shot out and grabbed the big man by the front of his shirt, catching him off guard and pulling him towards him. 'Listen,' he hissed, his voice icy with menace, ears alert for every sound that would tell him what was happening outside. 'Do you want to die?'

Bull Bulcombe's big brutal face turned an ashen grey. 'No,' he choked, twisting his head to one side, as if he were being strangled, 'No, I don't want to die . . . but I won't fly this goddam plane—'

With his free hand, Stuermer pressed his pistol to the big man's temple. 'Then you will die and one of the others *will* fly it. Make no mistake of that. One of the three of you will fly this plane in the end.'

'Hold on, Bull,' Prof cried. 'The Kraut's talking a load of crap! He doesn't—'

Ox-Jo rammed the butt of his machine-pistol in the little wounded gunner's stomach and he went down, with a gasp, onto the littered metal deck like a gasping, stranded fish.

Stuermer curled his finger around his trigger, the knuckle white with pressure. 'I'll give you to three,' he growled. 'Then if you don't do as you are told, it will be the next one. *ONE!*'

Bull Bulcombe's eyes rolled about in a terror: his breath came in short shallow gasps. Outside the snap and crack of the small arms intensified again and Stuermer knew instinctively that the Americans were preparing to rush the Edelweiss positions once again. Soon Greul would have to fall back. Now it couldn't be more than fifteen minutes before the charges started going off.

'TWO!'

'Fellas,' Bull sobbed. 'What am I gonna do?' Tears streamed down his ashen face now. 'He's gonna kill me! Tell me!'

'Hold on, Bull,' the second pilot gasped through gritted teeth, his eyes blazing with anger in the yellow light of the crowded cockpit. 'The Kraut wouldn't dare kill you in cold blood here, when he knows that we're gonna take him—'

'THREE!' Stuermer rasped and prepared to fire, to blast the big American violently into eternity.

'NO!' Bull screamed, completely broken now, 'I'll do it! No, don't shoot . . . I'll fly her!'

Stuermer waited for no more. He dropped his pistol, feeling the sweat trickle down his spine unpleasantly, and swung round on a relieved von Ernst. 'All right, he's all yours. I'll give you ten more minutes before I pull back. You're on your own now. *Hals und Beinbruch!*' And with that he was doubling down the ladder again into the glowing darkness to help face the new American attack.

'What the devil?' Greul began, as the louder roar overpowered that of the massed jeeps advancing on the waiting defenders crouched below the Liberators.

'Light plane!' Stuermer yelled in warning, as he flung himself panting into the sand next to Greul.

Above them, at less than fifty metres, a small light plane came zooming in. A light flicked on, and pinned them to the ground with its brilliant blinding beam.

'Look out!' someone screamed frantically, as a dark figure leaned out of the side of the plane. A machine-gun chattered frenetically. Scarlet flame stabbed the darkness.

A trooper flung up his arms, and screaming in his death agony, hit the sand.

Stuermer cursed and fired a wild burst. But the plane was already zooming out of range, coming round, obviously for another attack, while the menacing army of jeeps came ever closer.

Stuermer made a quick decision. They would have to abandon the Liberators in the hope that their plastic explosive would go off before the Americans could de-fuse the time pencils. 'Pull back . . . *for Chrissake, pull back!*' he screamed as the light plane came roaring in once more, the machine-gun chattering from over its side.

The men needed no urging. They ducked beneath the shelter of the Liberators, hearing the slugs howl off their armoured parts and rip great holes in their own softer skin. Another trooper went down and another. Stuermer slung his machine-pistol and grabbed the nearest man, whose knee-cap had been shattered. 'Hang on, comrade,' he gasped, blinded by the massed lights of the jeeps as they bolted over the desert. He put his arm under the wounded trooper and started to drag him after the rest.

'They're bugging out . . . *the Krauts are bugging out*!' a powerful, authoritarian voice bellowed metallically through a megaphone.

Stuermer did not understand the words, but he knew instinctively the Americans had seen they were pulling back. He struggled on.

Now they were clear of the Liberators, the light plane came howling in at less than ten metres. A shower of light grenades trumbled among the fleeing Edelweiss men. They exploded everywhere in a fury of bright blue flame. Shrapnel hissed through the air frighteningly. Men howled as they were hit. Others flopped to the sand soundlessly. They would get up no more.

Next to Stuermer the wounded trooper gasped. It seemed to come from deep within him. Stuermer felt the man stiffen like young children do when they are in a midst of a tantrum. 'Come on, comrade . . . come on!' he urged desperately. 'Only a few more metres. Look the plane—'

'Can't . . . can't make it, sir,' the man choked, the blood spilling from both sides of his mouth in an uncontrollable stream. 'Had it, sir. Let me go . . .' Suddenly with the last of his dying energy, he cried, splattering the front of Stuermer's shirt with bright red blood, 'Piss off! Can't you let me die in peace. PISSS . . .' the words died in his mouth, as he drowned in his own blood. Stuermer let him drop and staggered after the others.

The first of the pursuing jeeps were nosing their way through the line of the Liberators, getting ever closer to the fleeing survivors. Here and there a trooper knelt and fired a quick burst at the advancing Americans before turning and running towards the Liberator that von Ernst had picked for their escape.

'Close in on them, men!' that impersonal metallic voice boomed through the megaphone, above the roar of the light plane and hectic rattle of the machine-guns. 'Come on . . . *close in now, I say*! . . . Out, you crew chiefs and check them out!'

Now, the second wave of jeeps braked to a halt in a flurry of sand and the mechanics in the oil-stained overalls and peaked khaki caps, armed with torches, started to swarm among the abandoned Liberators like so many huge fireflies looking for the signs of sabotage.

They didn't get far. Suddenly there was a thick muffled crump. A mechanic screamed. Dropping his torch, he held up his hands to protect his face. To no avail. The undercarriage of the Liberator that he was examining disappeared in a burst of smoke and it collapsed on the screaming man like a great broken-legged silver bird.

Next to it another charge exploded. The fuel tank burst and spread angry red flame, tinged with oil, in a frightening, roaring sea across the sand.

In an instant, the nearest jeep was engulfed in it. A lone man ran screaming from it, flames racing up his body, consuming it as he ran, until he fell writhing in the desert, a terrible, whimpering human torch.

Plane after plane went up in flames. From the other side of the base, there came the sound of the alarm gongs. Fire sirens started to wail. Powerful engines raced. The metallic voice roared urgently, 'Halt . . . everybody back to the B-24s! Get on the stick . . . Let's defuse those time bombs . . . *ON THE STICK NOW!*'

Abruptly, the whole American attack ended in complete confusion: some Americans fled madly to their jeeps to get away from the explosions and the sea of flame speading everywhere; others braved the flames and raced to prevent more of the terrible little charges exploding; and the huge fire engines shrilled their way across the desert, their white-clad crews hanging on for dear life, heading straight for the conflagration.

For a few moments the hard-pressed survivors, many of them limping and wounded now, had a respite. While Greul and Stuermer stood guard, routinely pumping quick bursts to left and right, they filed by the two officers and clambered up the straight ladder, leaving a trail of blood behind them on the rungs.

Then it was Stuermer's and Greul's turn. They fought their way up the ladder, now sticky and slippery with human blood, and blinked as they were struck by the yellow and green lights of the cockpit. Stuermer breathed a quick sigh of relief. Everything seemed under control. While their prisoners crowded the far end of the tremendous machine, Ox-Jo and Jap manned the machine-guns, facing the direction of the American attack. And von Ernst, pistol levelled, stood over a sweating, terribly frightened Bull Bulcombe, who was flicking a myriad of complicated switches while his gaze flashed from one green-glowing control dial to the other.

Von Ernst managed to raise a grin, although he, too, knew the seriousness of the situation. They had only minutes to take off, without any aid from the tower and under American fire, before the enemy would rush them again. 'All fucked up, sir,' he reported in a mock military tone, using the old soldier's expression, 'situation normal!'

Stuermer returned his grin momentarily and said, 'Has it ever been different, Lieutenant, in the Greater German Army?' Then he helped to bundle the wounded to the rear of the plane where they could take over the guarding of the Americans from their unwounded comrades.

They had successfully managed to reach the Liberator after sabotaging an estimated fifty planes. The big, four-engined crate looked so powerful, so impregnable. Yet, a worried Stuermer knew, too, that if they didn't get off the ground soon, the bomber could well be a death trap, a coffin of blazing metal. For what was left of Stormtroop Edelweiss, time was running out. *Fast* . . .

FIVE

Bull Bulcombe hit the button.

Around him in the blood-stained, débris-littered mess of the Liberator, the survivors of Edelweiss tensed, the racket coming from outside forgotten momentarily.

Nothing!

The big American made as if he were about to turn in the pilot's seat. Von Ernst didn't give him a chance. He dug the muzzle of his pistol brutally into the back of his right ear. 'Try again,' he commanded coldly.

'Oh, you rotten sonuvabitch!' a still defiant Prof cried from the rear-end of the tense, silent plane.

A sweating anxious Bulcombe, his face an unnatural green hue in the reflected lights of the controls and the fires burning everywhere outside, did as he was ordered.

There was a throaty cough, a strange, high-pitched whine, a splutter of the first engine beginning to backfire.

Von Ernst beamed at Stuermer and kept the pistol pressed hard at the back of Bull's sweating neck, as the first engine roared into noisy life.

Bull pressed the switch of the next engine and the next, until they were all roaring away, the rev-counter needles flickering madly, the whole great fuselage trembling violently.

Stuermer forgot the pilot for a moment. 'Everything not needed, overboard now!' he commanded. 'Rations, packs, weapons – throw it out quick. We need all the altitude we can gain.'

'Weapons?' Greul queried.

'Yes weapons,' Stuermer snapped in answer. 'We'll keep these machine-guns here,' he slapped the one in the blister nearest to him, manned by an anxious Jap. 'And any of the crew's kit – rations and the like you can find. Come on, jump to it. We'll be taking off in a minute.'

'What about the prisoners?' someone called over the roar of the four engines. 'They're only unnecessary ballast now.'

Stuermer considered for a moment. No, they would be useful for one particular reason, now that they had partially succeeded in their mission. 'Keep them. We will have need of them in due course. All right, get on with it!'

Now as Bull revved the four engines, feathering them carefully as he prepared to take off, the unwounded survivors started to litter the desert below with the unnecessary items.

Stuermer turned his attention to the pilot. 'Have you got enough petrol to get us to Sicily?' he snapped.

Bull nodded and swallowing hard said, 'She's all gassed up for the—' He caught himself in time, but Stuermer knew what he meant. He had studied the Liberator's capabilities. In order to fly the mission to Ploesti and back safely, she would need in the region of 12,000 litres of petrol. It was far too much, but they couldn't ditch it till they were airborne. 'All right,' he commanded. 'Roll the plane onto the runway and let's get airborne.'

'But it ain't as easy as that,' Bull began to protest, but a harsh jerk from von Ernst's pistol choked it off. He thrust forward the controls and the huge bomber began to roll forward slowly, trailing a tremendous wake behind it, the reflected light of the fiercely burning fires colouring the anxious faces of the Germans and Americans inside an eerie crimson.

They bumped onto the tarmac. The plane's speed began to increase. From the direction of the tower a machine-gun opened up. Tracer spat their way. Ox-Jo pressed the trigger of his heavy machine-gun. It hammered into murderous activity. Suddenly the cabin was full of the stink of burnt cordite. Shells rattled to the deck in yellow glittering profusion. The m.g. at the tower ceased abruptly. Ox-Jo raised his hands above his head in the manner of a boxer who has just scored a knockout. 'What da ya say to that?' he chortled, to no one in particular.

Jap snorted and said with a sneer, 'Aw, go and crap in yer hat! That's nothing. Easy as falling off'n a log. Now watch this.' He squatted behind the heavy machine-gun and swung it from left to right. Without appearing to take any aim, he fired three quick controlled bursts. A group of Americans lining up on the top of the radar shack, armed with M-1s and Tommy guns, were swept from the roof, as if they had been swatted from it like a bunch of flies. The Liberator rolled on.

Now it was beginning to gather speed at a tremendous speed. The lights and patches of darkness started to flash by like those of a station glimpsed from a high-speed express train. Signal flares rose into the air directly to the plane's front. 'They're ordering us to stop!' Bull Bulcombe yelled above the roar of the four racing props.

'And *I'm* ordering you to keep going!' von Ernst cried.

A truck hove into view, racing straight for the track. Above the cockpit in the upper turret one of the troopers ripped off a burst from the machine-gun there. A trail of flying, blue sparks raced across the tarmac towards the truck – and missed. Next instant, the driver had flung himself out in a shallow dive and lay cowering in the drainage ditch, hands pressed over his ears, as the bomber bore down on him.

'The truck!' Stuermer yelled in sudden alarm. 'It's blocking the runway!'

Bulcombe saw the danger in the same instant. He grunted hard and heaved at the controls, his powerful shoulder muscles threatening to burst through the thin fabric with the strain.

Instinctively, Stuermer closed his eyes. They wouldn't make it, he knew they wouldn't. In a minute there would be a tremendous crash and the Liberator would be skidding across the tarmac without its undercarriage, a burning helpless wreck, a funeral pyre for Stormtroop Edelweiss.

The Liberator shuddered. One of the tyres exploded

with the noise of 88mm shell going off. Below the truck flashed by, keeling over under that impact, leaving the B-24 to stagger ever higher into the darkening sky.

Automatically, Bull pressed the undercarriage button. There was a whir as the electric motor started to haul it up. A metallic clang and it was in place, albeit with only one tyre still sound.

They were airborne. Von Ernst thrust his pistol in his belt and grinned in triumph at Stuermer who sat down suddenly, all strength gone from his legs. They had done it. They had gotten away. For the time being at least, they were safe . . .

'Continental Europe,' Bull explained grumpily as the big plane plodded on through the cloud, 'is divided into *Luftwaffe* defence zones. Down to the south there are six of them, each covering 115,000 square miles. Each of these is, in its turn, divided into a hundred different sectors. As soon as we approach Corfu, which is Sector 00 of Zone 24 East, we will be picked up by the *Luftwaffe* Fighter Command based on Otopenii north of Bucharest.'

'I see,' Stuermer said absorbing the information which had been given so unwillingly, and then asked, 'Are there any fields around there where a bomber of this size might land?'

Bulcombe shook his head firmly, not taking his eyes off the wet, white cloud through which they were now flying.

'What about Sicily?'

'Strictly *Luftwaffe* fighter and seaplane bases.'

'Mainland Italy?'

Bulcombe hesitated. 'North of Bari there is an Italian Air Force field. I've seen their Savoias land there. They're two engined bombers. But whether the runway there is long enough—'

'Make for Bari Field,' Stuermer cut him short.

'Okay, okay,' Bulcombe gave in, a virtually broken man now. 'But you know it ain't that easy. Even if we can get through our own fighters which will have scrambled by this time, you will have to face your own people, the *Luftwaffe* and the Eyeties, and I can tell you from personal experience, those wops fire first and ask questions afterwards – they are so damned trigger-happy.'

Stuermer ignored the objection. Instead he said, 'What do you do if you're crippled in action and want to surrender?'

Bulcombe thought for a moment. 'Well, on the odd mission that I've seen that happen, our guys usually lower their undercarriage as a signal to the fighter pilots that they are not prepared to fight anymore. That normally gets them a safe escorted landing to the nearest Kraut – er – German field.'

Stuermer dismissed the matter. 'All right, that is what you will do as soon as we spot one of our own planes.'

'And if it's one of ours?'

'Then, my dear Captain Bulcombe, you will have a grandstand seat, a unique opportunity to see the Greater German Army going into action.' He turned and swayed his way to the centre of the plane where the wounded lay, a few of them unconscious, but most of them awake and alert now that there was a prospect of their reaching the Homeland safely once more.

For a while he chattered with them, handing them pieces of American chewing gum taken from the prisoners and bits of rich milk chocolate of a kind they hadn't tasted for years. For smoking was strictly forbidden, as the reserve tanks were open, ready to be dumped soon. Then slowly the big plane was sliding out of the wet clouds into the new day, the sun already teetering on the horizon, with down below them the sullen green tossing sea – and the sinister black dots flying a parallel course to them.

'Fighters!' von Ernst whispered, almost as if the pilots so far below might hear them and be alerted, rubbing the sleep out of his red-rimmed eyes. 'Do you think they have seen us, sir?'

Stuermer lowered his binoculars which he had focused on the nine twin-boom Lightnings flying below, dragging their shadows behind them over the water. 'Don't think so – not yet at least.' Hastily he alerted the men manning the guns to be prepared for action, while Bull Bulcombe, very much aware of the personal danger he was in, threaded the plane in and out of the drifting cloud the best he could, trying to conceal the Liberator from the deadly hawks below, for as long as possible.

The minutes ticked by leadenly, the troopers who were not manning the guns were breathing with difficulty as Bulcombe edged their plane ever higher, into thinner air. Behind them the American wounded started to moan and call for oxygen.

Stuermer ignored them. There weren't enough masks and portable bottles to go round. In the final analysis the rest of them could black out; the oxygen masks would be reserved for the pilot, gunners and guards. He kept his gaze fixed intently on the fighters below, waiting for the first indication that they had spotted the bomber flying above them.

Suddenly the leader waggled his wings. Stuermer knew the signal and Bulcombe struggling with the controls put it into words for him. 'They're on to us!' he cried, thrusting the stick backwards into a steeper climb.

The fighters came zooming up. Tracer erupted from their wings. There was so much of it and it was so thick that it seemed like a great net woven of fiery cord. But it fell below them harmlessly and the gunners did not even reply. They knew that they were still out of range.

The Liberator shuddered and shivered. Now the men were grabbing at their collars, ripping them open, gasping for breath as the air became progressively thinner. Bulcombe looked at the mask hanging above his head. Stuermer nodded his agreement, his own chest heaving frantically. Bulcombe did not need a second invitation. He grabbed at it greedily and concentrated on taking the Liberator higher. The gesture was a signal for the gunners and the guards. They did the same, while the rest choked and gasped. Now the Lightnings were breaking up into an attack formation, zooming off to left and right, chivying for position. Stuermer knew they were going to be in for a fight. Every alarm bell in his brain and heart was ringing a lively warning. His nerves were steady but his brain raced rapidly. The fear was there and it was unpleasant, but it was bearable. Somehow, he knew, if they didn't lose their nerve, they would pull it off. They had not come this far, lost so many good men and suffered so much, to fail now. Besides the problem of Ploesti was not yet solved and now he knew he was the only man who could solve it.

He waited.

'*Here they come!*' Ox-Jo ripped off his mask and called, before clamping it to his mouth once more and grabbing his .50 calibre. The wounded and prisoners huddled frantically together. The others dropped to the deck as Ox-Jo and his running-mate Jap opened up simultaneously.

The noise was tremendous. Yellow-gleaming cartridges tumbled to the deck in their hundreds so that within seconds the two waist gunners were up to their ankles in them. Orange tracer like glowing ping-pong balls curved in frenzied zig-zags at the fighters. Stuermer flashed a look to starboard. A Lightning had been hit. Thick white fumes of glycol had begun to stream from one engine. Its nose sank. Next instant it was streaming straight downwards towards the sea.

But there were more. Abruptly, a great roar filled the Liberator. A door had been torn off. Stuermer fought the sudden wind which threatened to drag him from his seat. On the floor the wounded Americans and Germans screamed, as their soft bodies were further violated.

'Take her high for God's sake!' Stuermer cried desperately.

'She's too heavy,' Bulcombe's muffled voice came back as he fought the stick.

'The gasoline,' Stuermer gasped, his mouth pressed close to the American's ear. 'Release the gas!'

As one of the attackers walked his fire deliberately along the whole length of the B-24, chipping huge pieces of her silver fabric away, Bulcombe hit the control. There was the stifling stench of escaping petrol. Gasoline started to stream from the wing tank, falling away behind them and drenching a Lightning roaring into attack. Perhaps it was the fire from its cannon or perhaps it was simply the plane's hot engines which ignited the fuel. But whatever the cause, the Lightning was streaming down to earth the next moment, a mass of roaring flame.

'Two down, seven to go!' Ox-Jo cried uproariously, taking off his mask momentarily, before clapping it on again and swinging the heavy machine-gun round once more.

Gasping and choking as if he were on some high peak, Stuermer staggered to the blisters, lugging heavy belts of ammunition, and began to feed them alternatively into the machine-guns.

The Lightnings were coming in again, while Bull Bulcombe threw the great plane about, trying to evade the fighters. This time the Lightnings tried a new approach. Lowering their undercarriages so that their speed was lessened and they could keep the B-24 longer in their sights, they did some nice deflection shooting from some five hundred metres away.

Lines of holes were ripped in the Liberator's fuselage everywhere. Shattered metal flew through the air on all sides. The wounded, gasping and writhing for air on the floor, were hit again and again. Behind Stuermer, Jap cried, 'Hot damn shit, they've gone and shot me!'

Stuermer spun round. He ducked as another row of holes was stitched just above his head as if by some gigantic sewing-machine. Jap leaned weakly against the fuselage, blood seeping through his tightly clenched fingers.

Stuermer forced away his hand. Blood jetted out in a bright scarlet curve. The slugs had severed an artery. Hastily, he ripped off his American tie and set about making a tourniquet while Jap smiled up at him weakly, his face rapidly turning grey.

'Do yer think, sir, it'll get me a pension?' he asked thinly when Stuermer had finished.

'What do you want a pension for?' Stuermer cried, feeling his lungs flood with good air as the plane started to come lower. 'You'd only spend it on beer and women, you rogue.' He stepped over Jap and grabbed his weapon.

A Lightning, only three hundred metres away, was firing controlled bursts at the Liberator. 'Bastard!' Stuermer cried, tightening his grip on the twin handles, waiting for the Lightning to show him its belly. Up above him and to his rear, the unknown gunner and Ox-Jo started to hammer away. The noise was ear-splitting. Obviously the enemy was coming in that side, too. They were closing in.

The Lightning to his front must have thought that his friends were coming in too close for safety. He broke to the right suddenly. For an instant he made the fatal mistake of exposing his belly to the waiting gunner. Stuermer seized the fleeting opportunity presented him. The .50 calibre machine-gun pounded in his hands. White tracer hissed angrily at the Lightning.

With a great roar the Lightning exploded in mid-air. Stuermer ducked. Great fragments of gleaming silver metal flew in every direction, while the twin engines dropped to the ground whirling round and round like metallic leaves. A black lump came hurtling straight at a bemused Stuermer. He gasped. It was the body of the pilot, his knees tucked into his stomach. He flashed by so close that Stuermer felt he could have reached out of the open blister and touched him; he could even see a handkerchief flapping out of the pocket of his brown leather flying jacket. Then he was gone to be followed by a small round object, revolving frantically as it raced after the vanished body. Stuermer felt the hot bitter vomit fill his mouth at the sight. It was the pilot's head!

The fate of the third Lightning seemed to frighten the remainder off. Or perhaps they were beginning to run out of fuel. With a last few infuriated bursts of machine-gunfire, they broke off their attack and raced to the east. In a matter of moments they were black spots on the gleaming horizon. A moment later they were gone altogether.

Their attackers seemingly forgotten, the weary defenders of the crippled bomber started to help the wounded the best they could. In the shattered mess of the fuselage, old enmities were forgotten, as friend and foe looked to each other's needs.

Stuermer, wiping the sweat off his brow, feeling exhausted with the strain of that brief air battle, staggered over the groaning bodies and débris to the cockpit. 'What's the situation?' he croaked, telling himself he knew it already; it was terrible.

'Number three engine has gone completely,' Bull Bulcombe gasped, not taking his gaze off the myriad, flickering green needles, the back of his shirt black with sweat, rivulets of it running down his red neck. 'And number four's bound to go soon.'

Stuermer craned his neck and looked down. They were flying some five hundred metres above the Mediterranean. The white-capped waves and the green, heaving sea were clearly visible, but that was all. There was not a boat in sight, and the horizon was completely clear. Land was far away. He forced himself to ask the two overwhelming questions which were now uppermost in his mind. 'How far are we from land?'

Bull Bulcombe didn't take his eyes off the controls. 'About two hundred miles from Sicily.'

Stuermer nodded and converted the miles into kilometres. Sicily was some three hundred and twenty kilometres away. To Bari, it would be a total of – say – four hundred kilometres. Then he asked his second question. 'Do you think you'll make it?'

With some of his old brutal energy, Bull snorted, 'How the shit, should I know? Am I Jesus . . . do I walk across the goddam water?'

Stuermer turned. He had heard enough. Feeling the air inside getting appreciably warmer as the crippled bomber sank lower and lower, he stood in the middle of the fuselage, balancing the best he could. 'Listen everyone,' he said and then translated his words into English for the benefit of the Americans, 'we're going to jettison every last bit of unnecessary equipment, *including* weapons!'

'What if we are attacked?' someone cried in protest.

'We'll just have to take that chance,' he ordered. 'Now get to it. Rip the plane apart. Toss everything overboard. All right, now get to it!'

Feverishly, as the Liberator fell lower and lower, and Bull Bulcombe fought the controls, the men of Edelweiss tossed everything that was not absolutely essential overboard through the twin gun blisters.

Ox-Jo looked a little sadly at the big .50 calibre machine-gun and then, cradling it in his brawny arms, tossed it to the sea below. Now, the Americans began to help, too, explaining in a mixture of sign language and broken German what could be safely ripped from the interior of the Liberator, and jettisoned.

But still the crippled plane came lower and lower. Now the sea was less than two hundred metres below, and up front Bulcombe fought desperately to keep the plane flying as the second engine gave out and the right wing and its stalled propellers started to slide.

One of the other two American pilots struggled through the confused mess of the stripped fuselage to where Stuermer crouched. 'Sir,' he said very formally, his face tense and set. 'I've talked it over with the others. We're all in the same boat and so we've agreed to help. With your permission, I'll sit in as co-pilot for Bulcombe.'

'Bulcombe?' Stuermer echoed puzzled, then he realized it must be the name of the man at the controls. 'Yes,' he said hastily. 'By all means, thank you.'

Instinctively, the pilot said, 'You're welcome,' and then hurried forward and took his place next to Bulcombe. A moment later he, too, was sweating hard, as he fought to keep the plane in the sky, struggling to drag up the right wing which threatened to touch the water at any moment and drag them down for good.

Time passed in electric apprehension. The Americans and their German captors could do nothing but sit there and sweat it out, for Bulcombe had bellowed back from the controls that there should be as little movement as possible; it might upset the fragile trim of the plane now flying on two engines. To the rear, Shorty Perkins prayed in between stroking Jap's sweating brow, as the little half-breed snored in the harsh shallow manner of those drugged by morphine.

Behind the two pilots, Greul and Stuermer crouched, no longer guarding their prisoners, but intent on surveying the horizon for the first sight of land, sweating out the kilometres that still separated them from Sicily, as the Liberator scudded above the heaving sea, its remaining two engines coughing and spluttering alarmingly, spraying up showers of hot oil, as they bore the almost impossible strain.

'Land!' Greul gasped. 'Two o'clock . . . *land*!'

Stuermer swung his binoculars round. He was right. There was a faint brown smudge on the horizon to the right. 'Sicily!' he exclaimed. He pressed Bulcombe's damp, muscled shoulder, as if he willed him to make it. 'Come on . . . come on!' he hissed through gritted teeth.

They could now see the coast quite clearly, as the waves leapt up and seemed to touch their bullet-riddled belly. A stretch of bright white sand sprang into view. Bulcombe, seeming to read Stuermer's mind, snapped. 'No deal. Couldn't land the sonuvabitch there 'cos of them hills. We'd need more—' He stopped short as the third engine gave a frightening howl and the propeller suddenly ceased revolving.

The Liberator lurched alarmingly. Stuermer's heart stopped beating. They were going to crash into the sea! At the very last instant, the two pilots caught the plane and the engine stuttered and spluttered into action once more.

'Holy strawsack,' Ox-Jo called from the rear. 'Don't do that agen until I get my waterwings inflated.'

But no one had time for the big NCO's perverted brand of humour; now, even the veteran Edelweiss troopers – mostly Austrian and Bavarian Catholics – were joining in Shorty Perkins' prayers.

Land started to slip away underneath them, stretches of dark green olive woods intermingled with barren featureless mountain, which Stuermer knew would be no use for them. There was no alternative but to find that field at Bari or crash.

A city. Gleaming white buildings. A florid Baroque cathedral. People, staring up at them, shading their eyes against the glare of the sun. A convoy of mules running amok at the sudden roar of engines. A tower. Men in grey-green uniforms running for the anti-aircraft machine-gun positioned there. Tracer started to hurry towards them. Too late. They were gone. A gleam of water. Beyond more land. 'The Straits of Messina,' the co-pilot announced through gritted teeth, great glistening pearls of perspiration standing out on his forehead.

They flew over the narrow strip of gleaming water, the waves leaping up, as if eager and greedy to embrace them. Now and then they splashed up against the perspex momentarily obscuring vision for the two pilots.

Land again, with to the right the curve of a great port. 'Bari,' the co-pilot hissed. 'We bombed it last year . . . San Pancrazio, the Eyetie field is to the north of it.'

Stuermer nodded, watching the land whizzing up to meet them at a dizzy rate, kilometre after kilometre of densely packed olive trees and stunted firs. No sign of the field. Abruptly, the plane lurched. 'Port engine gone!' Bulcombe gasped.

'Start jettisoning more fuel!' the other pilot roared back and activated the pump.

The Liberator's nose rose slightly. Now they were brushing the tree tops, fighting desperately to keep the starboard and port wings parallel, exerting the last of their strength, gasping like men at the end of a long gruelling race, battling the unbalanced pull of the sole remaining engine.

The trees cleared. Some five or six kilometres to their front Stuermer could see a long stretch of concrete glittering in the sun. To left and right there were rows of camouflaged bombers lying behind protective bays of sandbags. It was the field!

'Here we go, Bull!' the co-pilot cried as the last engine coughed and failed and the plane gave an alarming lurch. 'We'll glide her in.'

Red flares started to erupt from the tower as the Italian controllers warned other aircraft to keep out of the way. 'Undercarriage won't go down,' Bulcombe cried struggling with the control. 'The whoreson must be jammed!'

The co-pilot fought the handpump. But it was no use! '*The hydraulic system won't work! Turn off the juice, Bull!*' he yelled, as the great bomber hurtled down at two hundred miles an hour, virtually out of control now. 'And the power. We don't want to go up in flames . . . *Belly-land her!*'

Bulcombe didn't answer; he was too pre-occupied. The marker lights were flashing by at a tremendous rate and the telegraph poles on either side of the field were now towering *above* them.

'Get the tail up, Bull!' the co-pilot screamed. 'It's our only chance to brake the bitch! . . . *Get that tail – UP!*'

Together, with the last of their combined strength, the two Americans heaved hard at the controls, desperately trying to pull the tail unit higher.

An Italian soldier in long red underwear burst out of a shack at the side of the runway and blasted away at the bomber with a shot-gun. The perspex cracked into a gleaming spider's web and blinded the two frantic pilots.

The bomber hit the tarmac. Stuermer gasped. Through a hole in the fuselage he could see the right wing engines hurtling by him. The plane sprang fighteningly into the air again. With their feet braced against the shattered instrument panel, their faces crimson, veins standing out like writhing cords at their temples, eyes bulging, the pilots pulled the control columns back hard against their heaving chests. They hit the ground again and immediately there was a tremendous screeching of protesting metal as the tail-piece hammered the tarmac behind them.

They slithered forward, red and purple sparks flying high in the air, bits and pieces of metal ripped off under that tremendous strain, the air filled with the stink of petrol and burnt rubber.

Stuermer held on for all he was worth. *Would they never stop?* He prepared his sweat-soaked body for the final crash – and oblivion. The tower flashed by. Everywhere Italian soldiers were springing into the drainage ditches on both sides of the runway as the huge bomber careened from side to side, completely out of control, heading for the ditch at the far end which would mean disaster and death.

Then slowly, but surely, their crazy skid across the tarmac slowed down, until finally the Liberator screeched to the left, hit some obstruction or other, slewed around in an awesome skid which sent the occupants flying right across the shattered, holed fuselage and came to a shuddering teeth-jarring halt facing the way it had come.

With legs that felt like rubber Stuermer clambered across the mess of the floor and stepped out of the door. For a moment he stared dumbstruck at the burn marks the length of the runway and the gleaming silver metal strewn everywhere. Men were running towards them, following an ancient, wood-burning truck. He tried to walk towards them. But his legs gave way and he sat down clumsily like a drunk.

Then they were suddenly surrounded by a happy, excited mob of dark-eyed Italians, slapping and kissing the bewildered, ashen-faced Americans and pointing ecstatically at the large white star on the Liberator's rump, yelling over and over again, *Liberazione! . . . liberazione . . .*'

Ox-Jo, slumped exhausted on the runway next to Colonel Stuermer, watched them with lack-lustre eyes and said, as the first German staff car nosed its way through the happy throng to enlighten them no doubt, 'You know what, sir . . . I think those shitting spaghetti-eaters think the Amis have come to liberate 'em!'

Stuermer smiled wearily, though the bitterness did not vanish from his blue eyes. It seemed a suitably absurd end to their impossible flight. He slumped back on the warm tarmac in the hot Italian sun and let it happen . . .

BOOK FOUR

TIDAL WAVE

Long, too long, America
Traveling roads all even and peaceful you
learn'd from joys and prosperity only
But now, ah now, to learn from crises of
anguish, advancing, grappling with direst
fate and recoiling not.
And now to conceive and show to the world
what your children en-masse really are.

Walt Whitman

On Sunday morning 1st August 1943 the *khamsin* came roaring in before dawn, flooding the coastal shelf with thick yellow dust so that the waiting Liberators stood in it like bathing elephants, howling like no wind of nature. It was an ill omen, but the thousands of men swarming over the Benghazi bases that morning, giving the engines a last clean, removing the dust from the bomb bays and machine-guns, had no time to think of such things. This was the day of Tidal Wave. The time for the great raid of Ploesti, which might knock Nazi Germany out of the war, had arrived.

Precisely at dawn, the crews, replete with bacon and eggs and much heavily-sugared coffee for extra energy, boarded their planes. Everywhere engines gasped and coughed and burst into life, flooding the cool dawn air with stinking, blue gasoline fumes and raising the dust on which no rain had fallen in four months, in thick clouds.

Exactly 712 engines roared as the first 178 planes queued up for take-off, each of them carrying 3,100 gallons of gasoline and 4,300 pounds of bombs, bullets and thermite sticks.

It was a tremendous weight and the first wave of aircraft, carrying more killing power than the whole Union and Confederate Armies at the Battle of Gettysburg, would be facing the suicidal problem of simply getting airborne.

At 0400 hours Greenwich Mean Time, the serious-faced middle-aged meteorologists stirred their tea-leaves for the final time and pronounced the weather favourable for an attack in the Balkans region. The tower controllers ran to the platforms and fired their signal pistols. The green flares hissed into the dirty white of the dawn sky, where they hung, bathing that vast armada in their sickly unnatural light before racing for the ground like fallen angels. One after another the heavily-laden monsters started to lumber forward to begin the seemingly endless run along the tarmac until finally, when it seemed that nothing would get them airborne, they left the ground, their undercarriages raising as they commenced their laboured ponderous climb to 2000 feet where they would join their attack formations.

The battle order started to shape up. There were the 29 pink ships of the first formation. Behind them came the green-painted planes of the Traveling Circus. Killer Kane's 47 lion-coloured Pyramiders followed. After Killer's planes there were the green Eight-Balls and, last of all, the 26 factory-fresh, gleaming silver planes of the raw Sky Scorpions, every man of their crew a novice and unblooded in battle.

Airborne at last, the groups started to form into Vs – three planes to each V – which possessed the firepower of 30 heavy machine-guns, more than three whole divisions of infantry in World War I. They streamed northwards dragging five miles of shadow behind them across the tranquil blue Mediterranean. It was a flying city of metal and glass. The men were able to talk to each other within the individual planes though strict radio silence had been ordered to avoid detection by the Germans. Steadily, the great formation of bombers began to eat up the long weary miles to their far-off destination in Rumania.

But already they had been picked up. In Athens, an excited German officer had commenced flashing out urgent signals to all defence commands in Southern Germany, Austria, Greece and Rumania, 'interested or affected'. *The Amis were coming at last . . . The Amis were on their way. The battle could soon commence . . .*

Within hours of their having crash-landed at the Italian air base, a plane-load of specialists from Berlin had flown in to debrief the survivors of Stormtroop Edelweiss and interrogate their prisoners. There had been men from Air Intelligence, staff officers from the Air Ministry, target specialists and three men in leather coats and black felt hats (in spite of the boiling heat), sent personally by *Reichsmarschall* Goering, who remained discreetly in the background, watching, waiting, biding their time. A weary Ox-Jo, lounging outside the interrogation building in the sunshine next to Stuermer had whispered under his breath to his CO, 'If you ask me, sir, they're cops, old style bulls . . . They've got Gestapo written all over their ugly mugs.'

By nightfall that same day, Air Intelligence had calculated that Edelweiss had only partially succeeded. They awarded them twenty Liberators destroyed, including the one they had escaped in, and a probable forty-two damaged on take off. As the severe-looking senior officer, who affected a pince-nez and seemed to have sinus problems, declared, 'The Americans will still have sufficient capability to launch a major raid on Ploesti. Our only hope now is to be able to find out when that raid will take place, so that we can concentrate *all* possible resources to meet it. *Reichsmarschall* Goering insists on that!'

The interrogators had gone to work with renewed energy on the prisoners, each one kept in a separate isolation cell from the others. All the old tricks and threats had been applied, but none of them had worked. Even the wounded, still untreated by the waiting Italian doctors, had stuck bravely to the old formula – name, rank, serial number – no more, no less.

About three o'clock that morning, the interrogators, their smart green-grey *Luftwaffe* uniforms, wrinkled and damp with sweat, had about given up. It seemed as if they would never get the date of the great raid from these stubborn fools of Americans. It had been then that the three middle-aged civilians had stepped in. They had flashed their silver 'dog licences' at the officers, who had suddenly turned pale at the sight of those official badges and muttered one frightening word, '*Gestapo!*'

The three of them – one very old and cadaverous who spat a lot and seemed in the final phase of some terminal disease; the second fat and pink and hairless who glistened like a freshly scrubbed pig; and the third, their leader, a leathery-faced middle-aged man with cunning dark eyes and a stump of unlit cigar gripped between the thick red lips of a sensualist or sadist – had already picked their victim. It was the same officer who Stuermer had selected as the most likely man to do his bidding, Captain 'Bull' Bulcombe.

'Come on, *los, du Ami schwein. Aufstehan* . . . GET UP!' the voice had seemed to come from a long, long way away.

But the fist which had smashed into the sleeping Bulcombe's face, when he had failed to react, was real enough. He had awoken with a start and flinched as he saw those three cruel faces staring down at him in the weak yellow light of the naked bulb in his bare cell.

'What—' he had begun. But an iron hard fist had smashed into his teeth and cut off his protest with brutal suddenness.

For a while the three of them concentrated on beating him up, pounding him almost routinely with their fists, and when he slumped half-conscious and bleeding to the floor, they used their boots on him until one of his ribs cracked audibly, and they, exhausted now, were leaning against the walls, their breaths coming in sharp harsh gasps.

The one with the pink piglike face, who seemed to be the only one who could speak English, gasped in an American accent. 'Listen I work in Milwaukee six years – beer brewery. No try to fool me . . . I know Americans . . . Now when the raid?'

Bull Bulcombe had stared pleadingly at those hard, sweaty faces, through puffed-up eyes, but there had been no mercy there. 'I can't . . . can't tell you that,' he said in a strangled voice, his neck twisted to one side, as if he were having the greatest difficulty in speaking.

A heavy fist clubbed down on the nape of Bulcombe's neck and he slumped down to the floor once more. They hauled him back to his feet again by his hair, and like boxers in some sleazy backstreet gym began punching him, slamming him back and forth between the three of them, the silence broken only by their heavy breathing, the thud of their fists on his broken bleeding flesh and his little yelps of pain at each fresh blow.

After what had seemed an eternity of burning, painful misery, the piglike one, with the sweat hanging like pearls in his hairline, snorted, 'Don't crap me, American . . . I ask questions . . . and I always get answer . . . Now when the raid?'

Bulcombe shook his head doggedly, not daring to open his mouth in case he blurted out the truth in his overwhelming fear, hanging on by virtue of a courage that he had never known he possessed.

The one who looked like a corpse snorted something angrily in German, while Bulcombe drooped there under the naked bulb, urine trickling down his trouser-leg unheeded, his face a swollen, bloody, blackened mess.

The one with the cigar, who was their leader, nodded his head thoughtfully, and said laconically, '*Ja. Ja. Machen wir* . . .'

Hardly aware of what was happening to him, Bulcombe felt himself seized and dragged down long, narrow, echoing corridors, his feet dragging, his face or his broken ribs punched cruelly whenever he seemed about to collapse.

Somewhere or other he had blacked out, but the shock of a pail of icy water thrown in his face had brought him to, eyes blinking, mind befuddled, unable to comprehend the strange rushing sound close by. Hands had seized him and he was half-carried, half-dragged to the source of that sound: a large open bath of the kind common to barracks all over Europe, the soldiers' communal tub.

He gasped and understood with a sense of wild, panic-stricken fear what the three men were going to do to him. New strength surged through his tortured body. Crazily, babbling like an idiot, he tried to free himself. To no avail. They held him in a grip of steel. Then with his mouth wide open and gasping, they thrust him face-downwards into the water. He gasped. He choked. Furiously, he squirmed and twisted like a madman, screaming silently as the water flooded his body. But there was no escape. A terrible roaring red wave submerged him. Stars exploded in front of his eyes and just when he felt that he must drown, the pressure was released and he found himself slumped on the tiled floor in a puddle of water and his own warm urine. He retched violently, vomiting blood and water, heart beating like a trip-hammer, gasping like a stranded fish.

They asked the old question once again. Bulcombe desperately wanted to answer it – he would have given his right arm to do so. But inside a harsh little voice snapped, 'Don't tell the Kraut bastards a thing. Stick it out Bull! Think of the guys back at base. *Not a goddam thing!*'

Numbly, not trusting himself to open his mouth in case he blurted out the date of Tidal Wave, he shook his head.

They grabbed him again. The side of his battered skull struck the side of the bath. His head rang. Blood-red stars exploded in electric profusion. Immediately, his lungs filled with water, now stained pink with blood. Bubbles raced to the surface. He threshed and writhed. He would drown in a moment. A great red roaring filled his ears, which were threatening to explode at any moment. *HE WAS DROWNING!*

He had talked, eventually. He had even pleaded with them to let him tell them *everything*. On his knees, hands clasped together in supplication like the child he had once tortured himself, a frantic pathetic broken wretch, who would have betrayed even his own mother to escape that terrible bath.

The words had spilled out of his broken-toothed mouth, while the three torturers had leaned against the wall happily, faces wreathed in cynical smiles, noting everything. '*Five stages . . . the rookies coming in the last group . . . assemble over Corfu . . . First Initial Point . . .*' and then the most terrible secret of all, the one that would mean the deaths of many hundreds of his comrades . . .' *date of attack, One August, 1943 . . .*'

Two hours later the sleeping camp was awakened just after dawn by the great echoing scream, the splintering of glass and the awesome smack of soft flesh slamming into hard concrete.

Stuermer was first out of the hut, rushing out into the fresh-scented, glowing morning. Bull Bulcombe twitched convulsively in his death throes, while from above the Gestapo men stared down open-mouthed from the shattered window.

He made a pretence of helping, as more and more men crowded around him, but instinctively he knew it was too late. Bulcombe was dying. The American's spine curved like a taut bowstring and he had half-raised himself, meaningless words coming from his ruined mouth. Then, with a sudden heart-rending gasp, he had fallen back. He was dead, arms flung out dramatically, poised in the red pool of his own blood.

Without another word, Stuermer, his fists clenched white in suppressed rage, walked away. He told himself that perhaps Bulcombe had not been thrown out of the upstairs window by his torturers but that in some last flickering of pride, he had flung himself to his death – voluntarily. It was a hope that he clung to ever afterwards, for without it everything seemed pointless. The human spirit *had* to prevail, come what may, or the human race might as well be wiped out there and then . . .

In the windowless, modern building which housed the *Luftwaffe* Fighter Command for Rumania, they knew that the planes the excited young officer had reported on their way from Athens were the ones they were waiting for. They were not heading for Southern Germany, Austria or anywhere else in the Balkans; they were aiming for Ploesti!

This was Operation Tidal Wave as the dead American prisoner had called it before he had died.

Now the 120 young *Luftwaffe* girls in their neat white blouses and black ties, all wearing headphones and facing the huge table map, started to mark in the location of each new plane identified by directing a narrow flashlight beam on to the map, while men climbed the ladders behind them to crayon it on the glass screens. All was controlled excitement, as the telephones jingled, the morse keys clattered and the mercury began to rise rapidly. It was going to be a very hot day, indeed . . .

The first group of fighters were racing in low for their 150-mile run. They would fly at almost tree-top height across the Rumanian plain until they reached the first initial bombing point. Like tourists watching from the windows of one of those first-class Pullman coaches that had rattled across these same plains before the war, the airmen stared at the sights: the waving peasants in traditional costume; the country girls in their stiff petticoat and floral headgear pausing in the harvest fields to wave at them with their wooden hay rakes; the heavy-bosomed, giggling schoolgirls bathing naked in the slow brown rivers. 'Hell fire,' they quipped happily among themselves, 'just shoot me down now and let me get at them broads!'

On and on they roared, totally unopposed, as they hurtled across that beautiful, green fertile plain, singing '*Roll out the Barrel*' and wolf-whistling the girls. '*This one was going to be a piece of cake!* . . .'

They came lower and lower, now racing across dizzy strips of alfalfa, tall, green corn and bright yellow bundles of the already harvested wheat. They began to draw together. The lead 22 Liberators were now flying wing-tip to wing-tip at fifty feet above the ground, blasting everything in their wake into a turmoil. They roared below the barrage balloons, linked to each other by chains, tethered there like silver elephants.

Suddenly, flak opened up – pink, green, red, black –

hissing way above the planes. The gunners were totally unnerved by this unexpected attack at this altitude. But they would get even with the German flak gunners, who had slaughtered the Liberators so many times before during high-level attacks. Concentrated machine-gun fire erupted from the ships. With a tremendous mechanical clatter they shot it out with their rivals, sweeping them off the roofs of the flak towers like so many flies, scything them away in a rain of steel, leaving behind them as they flew on a groaning, bleeding mess of dead and dying men in field grey.

But the enemy gunners had taken their toll, too. Several of the big planes were trailing ominous black smoke from shattered engines. Inside their flak-riddled fuselages, men bled to death among the hot, smoking cartridge cases, receiving ever new wounds as they lay on the deck, their screams and cries for help drowned by the noise of battle. Up front the pilots, roaring through a solid hail of white fire and drifting clouds of black explosive, saw glittering shards of aluminium and pieces of shattered plexiglass floating past them in the slip streams; the whole sky seemed full of pieces of damaged and dying planes.

The first Liberator went into its death throes. Twin scarlet streams poured from its burning engines. The pilot fought the nose up in order to gain altitude so that his crew could parachute out. The ship stalled. It seemed to hang in the sky, peppered with the black cotton wool of the flak, like a burning torch. With a great blinding flash it disintegrated.

A second Liberator ran into the balloon line. The chains ripped off its wings as easily as a hot knife slicing through butter. For a few fleeting seconds, the mutilated rump appeared to fly on, then abruptly, it keeled over and hissed to the ground like a meteorite, scattering dead bodies as it did so.

The first refineries loomed up out of the fog of war, but the lead ship, already stricken and afire, knew it had no chance of clearing the silver hill. At two hundred miles an hour, the Liberator smashed into the metal side of the refinery. It crumpled up like a banana skin and began to slither down the side of the oil tank. Not for long. Suddenly there was a series of angry sparks the length of the wall and in an instant with a tremendous whoosh like the sound of some primeval monster taking a gigantic intake of breath, the whole structure was a sea of roaring flames.

The planes had started skip-bombing the buildings everywhere. The bombs tore holes in the brick structures and carried on without exploding into the next building, like rats gnawing their way to a resting place.

Another Liberator lost its wings to the barrage balloons and went skidding down a main street, both wings dropping after it, until it disintegrated in a ball of white flame against the side of a petrol truck.

The slaughter went on and on, and then they were through, leaving behind them a sea of raging flame and thick, oil-tinged black smoke. Thirty-nine planes had entered that Valley of Death. Fifteen of them had emerged and all of them carried their cargoes of dead men, propped up at their machine, eyes staring into nothing, crumpled over shattered controls, bleeding to death in their locked-in turrets.

The fighters, collected and scrambled for this first day of August, from all over Southern Europe, Germany, Rumania, Hungary, Bulgaria and even Italy, were waiting for the survivors.

Automatically, their pilots flicked on the switches which electrically armed their cannon and machine-guns. With their red lights flashing, they zoomed in for the attack. The Americans took up the new challenge. The terrific defensive barrage of the massed .50 calibre machine-guns broke up the attack formation at their first pass. The fighters winged to left and right at 500 kilometres an hour. Some didn't make it. A Messerschmitt was churned up in the prop wash of one of the Liberators. The pilot lost control. He hit the ground and skidded to a crazy halt, his shattered tail high in the air. Another turned on its back, hung suspended in the sky for what seemed an eternity, and then roared downwards, its burning pilot frantically fighting his way out of the cockpit with hands that had already turned into blackened, charred claws.

But now the fighters started to reform. This time they would not attack in a massed formation. They would come in cautiously in pairs, two to each Liberator, picking off those which were crippled and lagging behind, cut off from the protection of the massed machine-guns. The slaughter of the first group had commenced.

Now it was high noon. The Battle of Ploesti was fifteen minutes old. Below in the smoke-shrouded valley, three refineries were ablaze and Stuermer and the survivors of the mission to Africa, who had been specially flown to Ploesti in Goering's own personal plane (complete with a gold-fitted bathroom), to view the attack, could see that the Amis had knocked out at least half-a-dozen flak towers. Yet, they knew, too, from their briefing that Goering and his generals of the *Luftwaffe* had several other unpleasant surprises in store for the Americans as the shrill wail of the sirens indicated that more of the giant bombers were racing in to the attack.

Now Killer Kane's Pyramiders were roaring in, crewed by veterans, each one of them a man who had flown at least fifteen combat missions over Nazi-occupied Europe. These were the élite. The challenge had been taken up.

As had the others, they came zooming in at tree-top height, confident that the first group had plastered the flak defences. They were in for a surprise. As they hurtled towards the refinery, using a railway line as a guide, they overtook a speeding goods train. Some of the bomb-aimers were tempted to attack it; it was such an easy target, only fifty feet below. But their pilots ordered them sternly not to waste their bombs on such an unimportant target; they were after the refineries.

So the antiquated Rumanian goods train with its boxlike

freight wagons rolled on, directly between the two waves of flying giants which flanked it on both sides.

Away in the hills above Ploesti, Stuermer and the rest watching the strange combination through their glasses, held their breaths; they knew the purpose of that innocuous-looking goods train.

Suddenly, the hatch covers were ripped away from the sides of the freight wagons. Ugly-looking quadruple flak cannon flashed into view, their helmeted crews madly whirling their wheels and dials around, ready for action.

Kane to the left flank spotted them in the same instant that a tremendous blast of 20mm tracer shells struck the Pyramiders. He broke radio silence as the air all around filled suddenly with exploding shells and the big four-engined plane bucked and rocked under the detonations like a crazy horse, 'All ships,' he gasped, frantically trying to keep the Liberator on course, 'hold formation. Gunners, you tackle the train . . . *For God's sake hold formation!*'

Now a strange battle took place as the Liberators raced through the seething wall of whirling brown smoke towards the holocaust. From both flanks the sweating gunners fought their opposite numbers down below in the speeding train. Men everywhere were going down. A gun crew caught by the concentrated fire of a V were swept right through the open door of the other side of their wagon and slammed dead into the track beyond. A Liberator caught in the full blast of a quadruple cannon had its right side blown away, every crew member within range killed or fatally wounded, leaving the pilot, the sole survivor, to fly the ghost ship on towards the target.

Abruptly, the Americans struck lucky. Just as the lead ships spotted the cracking plant – a vital part of the oil refining process – through a break in the violent turbulent black clouds, a salvo of incendiary bullets hit the locomotive. Its boiler exploded with a spectacular roar, lifting the heavy engine right off the track and slamming it down again, its back broken. The train came to an abrupt halt. The Liberators flew on, many of them streaming thick black smoke now, leaving the gunners behind, waving their fists at the departing Americans in impotent rage.

Killer Kane plunged into the seething smoke, the sweat trickling down the small of his back, wet and sticky, as he realized just how narrow their escape had been. But he didn't realize yet the number of casualties. They had dropped their bombs all right, but they would never escape this holocaust.

They were through now, and beyond the Messerschmitts lined up to take them on. Those of the gunners who were still alive sprang to their weapons as the survivors tried to close their formation into a defensive V.

The slaughter commenced once more. A gunner standing on one leg – his other had been severed and lay below in a pile of cartridge cases – caught a German fighter in the belly with a long burst. The Messerschmitt came apart, like a dropped jigsaw puzzle. A Liberator, its right wing scraping the ground as it staggered on, was attacked by four fighters. Confident that this one couldn't escape them, they peppered it at sixty yards' range. The fuselage was full of choking white puffs of smoke like fireworks exploding. The Liberator's ammunition began to detonate, zigzagging in crazy white spurts around the dying bomber. Up front, the pilot, one eye shot out, the armoured shield to his back riddled with the bullets which had ripped his back open, heaved back the controls in sudden dying fury. The Liberator came up. He kicked the rudder hard. By some miracle the bomber responded. To the right, the black-painted Messerschmitt, its undercarriage down to decrease speed, stopped firing. Instinctively, the German realized what his dying American opposite number was going to do. Frantically, he tried to raise his undercarriage. Too late. The giant bomber slammed into him. He disappeared. Locked together in a fiery embrace of death, friend and foe hurtled to the earth.

The Pyramiders were crashing everywhere, the burning sky was full of their drifting white parachutes, their bodies and shattered bits of equipment. The fertile green

Rumanian fields were littered with the drifting smoke of their funeral pyres. On the ground, men were still dying, blinded, mutilated, thrashing impotently in the burning wreckage, trying to escape the fiery death traps the Liberators had become, cutting and sawing off their own limbs in a frantic attempt to get away before it was too late, their nostrils full of the stench of burning human flesh.

And then the survivors of Killer Kane's Pyramiders were through. The Butcher Bill had been terrible. Half Kane's bombers had been shot down over the target. Another twenty-five per cent wouldn't make it home. Now as they started to claw their way up into the Transylvanian Alps, fighting for altitude, feeling grateful for the thermal updraughts that would give them the benison of height, a grim-faced shaken Kane ordered 'Spring-cleaning!'

His crew knew what he meant. Into the slip stream went ammo belts, ration cans, precision tools; they even threw out their oxygen bottles. All that remained now were their parachute packs. Terribly hurt, completely unarmed, the survivors, many of them ominously trailing smoke, started to limp away into the mountains. The killing was over at last. Operation Tidal Wave was over.

Stuermer sat in numb silence on the hillside, with the rest of them. The spectacle which had just registered on his eyes was so fantastic that his brain had become frozen to the reality of the death and destruction below. If it had not been for the urgent squeezing of his guts, which were trying to purge themselves of the horrors he had just seen, he might well have been watching this week's version of the *Deutsche Wochenschau.*[1] Even Greul, that fanatical National Socialist, had been awed into silence by the terrible price they had forced the Americans to pay for their great attack.

In silence they watched as another B-24 died in the air; sinking ever lower, fighting to the very last, its port engine

[1] Wartime German newsreel.

screaming in agonized little bursts of power, it coughed again and came spluttering in for its final dive, oil streaming from its shattered engine.

They ducked automatically, as it shot over their heads, the two pilots dead at the controls, the white horrified blurs of the blister-gunners' faces staring out at them as the doomed ship carried them to their inevitable fates.

Stuermer waved his hand, 'Follow me,' he said tonelessly.

The handful of men in the field-grey of the Alpine Corps plodded after him into the hills, each man wrapped in the cocoon of his own thoughts, their backs at last turned to the holocaust below. They forgot the burning planes and the grotesque, butchered bodies of their crews, with their dead lips drawn back wolfishly from their gleaming teeth, or the dumb horror of the corpses swaying back and forth by their parachutes from the trees. For a while they dismissed the brutal reality of man's ability to destroy. Their pace quickened, as they left the acrid smoke behind them and began to enter the cleaner air of the mountains – their true home.

Stuermer paused and let them file by him silently. He savoured their honest, weary, bronzed faces, and felt the deep bonds of affection that existed between him and them. They plodded on into the mountain sun.

For a while he stood there, watching them go. Tidal Wave had failed. The Americans would not come again. Hitler's war would continue for a little while longer. Soon it would embrace them once again in its awesome deadly grip. Stormtroop Edelweiss would have to fight another day, of that he was sure. But for the time being, they would savour their time out of war, high in these remote Rumanian mountains, the vulgar pomp and brutality of the brown creed forgotten temporarily.

He was filled with a sudden warmth, a kind of happiness. Most of them had survived, unlike those hundreds of young men in the khaki who had died so violently this August day. Stormtroop Edelweiss had survived! New energy flooded his weary body and he felt imbued with fresh resolve and energy. 'Hey,' he cried, his cry echoing and re-echoing among the snow-capped glistening peaks. '*Hey Stormtroop Edelweiss, wait for me . . .*'

TO THE FALLEN OF PLOESTI

To you who fly on forever, I send that part of me which cannot be separated and is bound to you for all time. I send to you our hopes and dreams that never quite came true, the joyous laughter and showery tears of our boyhood, the marvellous mysteries of our adolescence, the glorious strength and tragic illusions of our young manhood. All these that were and perhaps would have been, I leave in your care, out there in the Blue.

John Riley 'Killer' Kane, U.S.A.F. (Ret)